WINTERLING

Sarah Prineas

WINTERLING

HARPER

An Imprint of HarperCollinsPublishers

Library of Congress Cataloging-in-Publication Data
Prineas, Sarah.
    Winterling / Sarah Prineas. — 1st ed.
        p.   cm.
    Summary: Spirited young Fer travels through the Way to a mag-
ical world in which beings part human and part animal serve an evil
ruler known as the Lady, and where she hopes to learn about her
long-lost parents and her own identitiy.
    ISBN 978-0-06-192103-2 (trade bdg.) — ISBN 978-0-06-
192104-9 (lib. bdg.)
    [1.   Magic—Fiction. 2.   Identity—Fiction. 3.   Shape-
shifting—Fiction. 4. Fantasy.] I. Title.
PZ7.P93646Win   2012   2011019974
[Fic]—dc23   CIP
                                                        AC

Typography by Andrea Vandergrift
12 13 14 15 16   LP/RRDH   10 9 8 7 6 5 4 3 2 1
❖
First Edition

To Jenn Reese.
For you, and for the girl you once were.

prologue

The dog fled. He raced down a shadowy forest trail lit by the full moon. Hearing the howl of the wolves that pursued him, he left the path for the darker forest, struggling through brambly bushes, dodging trees that grabbed after him with long, twiggy fingers.

A stream, or running water to throw the wolves off his scent—that's what he needed.

On he ran, panting with the effort.

The Mór demanded loyalty from all her creatures. He was bound against his will to serve her, but unlike the others who served her, he could see what she truly was. When she had ordered the hunt of one of her own people, he'd refused. He'd been stupid—*stupid*—and now he was the one they hunted.

The wolves howled again, closer.

They were going to catch him. And when they did, they would kill him, if that was what the Mór willed.

He was stumbling now, nearing exhaustion. Then he heard the rush of water over stones, smelled the fresh scent of water—a stream. He made for it, gasping for breath, his tongue lolling.

The water felt cool on his scratched paw pads. He stumbled up the stream until it got too deep, then scrambled out and found the path that ran alongside it. From behind he heard the *yip* of one wolf calling to another, and then they were there, rushing like gray shadows from the dark forest, surrounding him.

Snarling, he ducked away, and a wolf lunged and raked its fangs across his shoulder. He ran, feeling the burn of the wound, and they pursued. One wolf bounded alongside him and slashed at his foreleg, then fell back.

Despairing, he limped along the narrow path, seeing light ahead, an opening in the forest where the stream flowed into a perfectly round pool that reflected the full moon overhead. With a last, desperate bound, he leaped for the pool, the wolves surrounding him, snarling, biting, their teeth bitterly sharp.

He expected water, and then a bloody death.

Instead, he fell through the pool into darkness deeper than any night he had ever known.

one

The girl named Fer edged up to the kitchen door. Overhead, the night sky was spangled with stars, except for a brighter patch where a crescent moon, just as thin as a fingernail paring, hung over the bare branches of the oak trees along the driveway. The kitchen windows shed their light over the wiry brown grass of the backyard. At the edge of the yard, Grand-Jane's white-painted beehives were lined up, the bees inside them asleep and quiet.

Winter had ended. Fer could feel spring coming in the smell of rich dirt, in the cold, knobbled nubs at the tips of tree twigs. Soon the oak trees would have mouse-ear-sized leaves budding out, and the bees would be stirring. Spring tingled just under her skin, waiting to burst out.

But now everything was waiting. It was just this chilly in-between time. Mud time.

Fer shivered and put her hands into the pockets of her patchwork jacket. In the left pocket, she had two twigs and a smooth stone she'd found in a creek that afternoon. In the right pocket, a little cloth bag of herbs, loose-strife and lavender, mugwort and harewort, a protective spell that her grandma made her carry with her always. Protection against what, she didn't know, and she didn't bother asking anymore. Grand-Jane's answer was always the same—a dark, silencing look.

Fer sniffed the air. The crisp smell of toasted noodles and onions; Grand-Jane had cooked a tofu casserole for dinner.

Mmm, dinner. Fer's stomach growled. She huddled into her patchwork jacket and shivered. She was awfully late. It would be even worse if the principal had called. Fer didn't mean to get into fights at school, but sometimes they just *happened* and there didn't seem to be anything she could do about it.

When she went in the door, Grand-Jane was going to have a conniption. A really hairy one.

Oh well, might as well get it over with. Fer went up the steps and into the kitchen.

At the sound of the door closing, her grandma, at the stove, turned and glared. Carefully she set down a covered casserole dish. "What time is it."

It wasn't a question. Grand-Jane knew what time it was. Fer glanced at the clock that hung on the wall beside the fridge. "Seven thirty-five?"

"Oh, for crying out loud," Grand-Jane muttered. She closed her eyes and took a deep breath.

Fer hunched her shoulders, ready for the shouting.

Grand-Jane released her breath and opened her eyes. "We have been through this, Jennifer," she said sharply. "It is not safe for you to be outside alone. You must come home immediately after school."

"I can't," Fer said, staying by the door.

"Yes, you can," Grand-Jane said.

No, she couldn't, not after being cooped up all winter. House, bus, school, bus, house. The same thing every single day, except on the weekends when it was just house, house, house, because she and her grandma never went *anywhere*. She had to get out under the sky or she got so twitchy, she felt like she might twitch out of her own skin.

Grand-Jane looked her over with sharp blue eyes. "And your school's principal called. Apparently you had a run-in with that Torvald boy again."

Not just Jimmy Torvald, but his brother Richie and their stupid friend Emily Bradley. *Jenny Fur-head* they called her. What was she supposed to do? Let them call her that? Her hair did come out of its braid and it did get messy, and sometimes it did get twigs tangled in it, but that was no reason for them to be so *mean* all the time.

"Well, Miss Sullen, tomorrow's Saturday," Grand-Jane said. "You'll spend it with me cleaning the stillroom." She turned to the stove, put her oven mitts back on, and carried the casserole dish to the red-painted kitchen table. "Take off your coat," she said, her back to Fer. "And come eat your dinner."

Fer started to unbutton her patchwork jacket, then paused. All day tomorrow cleaning the stillroom? That meant dusting shelves, sweeping out spider webs, sorting through hundreds of tincture jars and bags of crumbling herbs, and more lessons on herbology and healing spells. *And* Grand-Jane's sharp eyes watching her the whole time, as if Fer were about to burst into flames and her grandma had to be there, just in case, to dump cold water on her.

Grand-Jane's warm, red-and-yellow kitchen closed around her. Fer felt like a bird bashing itself against the walls of a box.

Quick as thought, before Grand-Jane could turn around, Fer opened the door and flung herself back out into the night.

She'd never been out this late before. The world felt different under the sliver-silver moon. The fields were more empty. The shadows were deep and mysterious. As Fer ran along the edge of the long driveway that led away from her grandma's house, her footsteps sounded loud, *crunch-crunch-crunch*-ing on the gravel. The chilly night air went into her lungs and made her feel lighter, almost like she could fly. She ran past the twin rows of oak trees lining the driveway. Then down the road a long way until she got to a stream that cut through a muddy field, slowing down now because the footing was tricky along here. Across another road and through a patch of scrubby forest.

This wasn't wild forest, it was just a strip of trees and bushes between two fields that, in the summer, would be rustling with head-high corn or dark green soybeans. In the distance, Fer saw the dark outline of a couple of silos and outbuildings, and the porch light of a farmhouse. Far away a dog howled, a lonesome moan that made the night feel darker, wilder.

Fer cut through the scrub, then picked up the stream again, panting now, and brushing hair out of her eyes.

The forest grew thicker. She'd gone this far before, but never at night. The trees were stalking shadows that reached for her with twiggy fingers, snagging her patch-work jacket. She stumbled through long, damp grass and, as the forest grew even thicker, rotting logs and drifts of dead leaves. She ducked around another tree, and the ground disappeared from under her feet.

Down she fell, tumbling through brambles and leaf-less bushes, bumping her knee on a tree root, grabbing for branches to stop herself, finally coming to land half in a stream.

Catching her breath, Fer climbed out of the water. Her pant leg was wet, and one arm of her jacket. She shivered and looked around. Where was she? The crescent moon had climbed higher in the sky and stood directly overhead. Fer had good night vision; the moon's thin light was enough to see by. She was in a deep ravine, one crowded with bare trees and bushes, the air cold and damp, as if all the chill from above had gathered here in this low spot.

Might as well see where the stream led. Water squishing in one of her sneakers, Fer followed the stream through the ravine, picking her way over slippery stones. The stream slowed, flowed smoothly over a shelf of rock, and then widened to form a pool in the middle of a clearing.

Stepping lightly, Fer walked around the pool. It was perfectly round, and springy moss grew right up to its edge. She stilled her breath, listening. Something in the air felt strange. Tingly, or twitchy, like a rope stretched too far and about to break. She knew what Grand-Jane would say, in her scoldingest voice: *Come home right now, Jennifer! It's not safe!* Fer felt in her pocket for the spell-bag of herbs and gripped it, the seam in the fabric rough under her fingers.

She gazed at the still, black surface of the pool. The moon was reflected there, not as the pale crescent in the sky above her head, but as a fat, full, yellow moon. How could that be? She knelt on the moss and leaned over the pool to touch it. The water felt cool and slick.

At her touch, the water grew mirror-still, and a slow tingle started in her fingertips. She held her breath, feeling a sudden, strange power fizzing under her skin. The tingle turned to an electric shock that sizzled up her fingers and through her body. She jumped to her feet. The fat water-moon shattered. Shadows surged from the pool, flinging drops of water that sparkled in the moonlight.

Fer stumbled back, tripping over a dead branch, and fell into a clump of brambles; their sharp thorns gripped her like clawed fingers and wouldn't let go. She heard snarling, then another sound that made the hair stand up on the back of her neck. Howling, like animals on the hunt.

Fer tore herself from the thorns and scrambled to her feet. On the other side of the shimmering pool, wolves, their gray fur silvered by the moonlight, circled a lump of shadow on the ground. The shadow snarled—it looked like a black dog—as one of the wolves darted in, its jaws snapping. The other wolves, two of them, swarmed around, and another plunged at the black dog. Fer heard a yelp of pain. The wolf leaped back, smiling with bloody fangs.

Three against one—not fair!

Without taking her eyes from the wolves, Fer groped on the ground for the thing she'd tripped over. *There.* A branch as long as her arm, with a jagged, broken-off end. Gripping her club, Fer raced around the edge of the pool, her feet slipping on the moss.

Swinging the branch like a baseball bat, Fer connected with the hindquarters of one wolf, which whirled and snapped at her; the other two wolves snarled and left the dark thing crouched in the shadows.

The three wolves advanced silently, their heads low, their fangs bared.

Fer held her ground and gripped her branch tightly. "Go away!" she shouted, and with her free hand felt in her jacket pocket for her bag of spelled herbs. She pulled it out and kept it clenched in her hand. One wolf lunged toward her and Fer stepped up to meet it, bashing her club across its muzzle. Fer swung the branch back and caught another wolf in the ribs, then jabbed the jagged end of the branch into the face of the third wolf. Still holding the spell-bag, she shouted, "Go away!" again, then a third time, and the wolves flinched back as if her words had more power than the club she swung, watching her from the corners of their eyes, fading back into the shadows.

Panting, Fer turned to the thing they'd been attacking. It had fallen beneath the branches of a bush; she saw its dark shape huddled there. Carefully, gripping her club in case it tried to bite, she pushed aside the branches, letting the moon's light in. Fer blinked and set down the club.

It wasn't a dog at all. It was a boy.

two

A figure swirling with power leaned over Rook, a Lady with wild, honey-colored hair waving around her head, and blazing eyes, holding a blunt stick for a sword. Rook flinched away, the shifter-tooth that he'd used to turn himself into a dog clutched tight in his hand. Then the Lady took her hand out of her pocket, dropped the stick, and suddenly she was just a girl wearing a patch-ragged jacket.

"Are you okay?" she asked, going to her knees.

Rook growled and edged away from her. Through the sharp pain of the wolf bites, he felt something else, something different. He wasn't in his own land. The moonlit pool, the fall through the darkness—the girl had opened the Way that went from his world to hers. That shouldn't have happened. What *was* she?

She reached out with a pale hand and touched his arm, right where it hurt most. Her fingers went away black with blood. "You're not okay," she muttered.

"Yes, I am," Rook spat out. The wolf-guards were wildlings—more like wild beasts than people. They were coming unbound from their oaths and rules when they were in their wolf form, but the girl's magic had sent them away. He could get back now, and maybe escape the hunt. "Leave me alone."

She pulled away from him, wiping her bloody hand on the moss. "I just saved you from those wolves, in case you didn't notice."

Yes, he'd noticed. Curse her, anyway. And curse the wildling wolves, too, them and their howling and their teeth sharp as daggers.

"They bit you," the girl said. She leaned closer, examining him. "There's blood all over," she said to herself. Then she nodded, deciding something. "Come on. I'll help you."

She was smaller than he was, but she was strong. She dragged him from the bushes to the moss that surrounded the Way.

"Did you see the—?" she started, then looked up at the sky.

Clouds had settled over the crescent moon; the pool

in the middle of the clearing glimmered pearly white.

"Never mind," the girl said.

The Way was still open, though, and Rook knew it'd stay open until she closed it. The girl *had* done it, brought him through to this other place where the air tasted strange and the ground felt wrong under his feet.

Climbing to his feet, Rook felt the gashes in his arms and the slashes over his ribs. His knees wobbled. Quickly he shoved the shifter-tooth into his pocket to join the shifter-bone hidden there.

"Here," the girl said, and took his arm over her shoulder.

He let her do it. His feet felt very far away, his head filled with shadows.

"Come on," the girl said. "I'll take you home."

* * *

The boy was still bleeding. His shaggy, black head hung down, and his steps wobbled. He leaned more of his weight against her.

Fer braced herself. She couldn't drag him up the steep side of the ravine, but if they followed the stream far enough they should come to a place where they could walk out.

With the moon hidden, the night grew deeper. The clouds lowered and a damp drizzle began to fall. Fer kept them to the edge of the stream. It was a shimmering darkness running between the flatter darkness of the trees and bushes alongside it. The stream rustled as it flowed, and a breeze made the naked tree branches *click-click-click* like dead bones.

"Keep going," Fer whispered.

They stumbled over rotting logs and thrashed their way through tangled bushes. As they were edging around a clump of wet brambles, the boy slipped on a patch of decaying leaves and gasped in pain.

Fer steadied him and looked around. There should be a path along here somewhere. She shifted the boy onto his own feet. "Stay here for a minute," she said.

"Do I look like I'm going anywhere?" the boy answered, his voice rough.

No, he looked as if he could barely stay on his feet. After steadying him with a hand on his shoulder, Fer pushed through the bushes, heading up the bank, away from the stream. After a few steps she found the path, a narrow deer trail fringed with dead grass. She knew where she was now. This part of the ravine ran through the Carsons' hay field. If they kept going, they'd hit a gravel road.

Fer slid back down the bank to where the boy stood leaning against a tree, his head lowered. "It's not far," she said, wiping damp hair out of her face. "Just up here."

She pushed him up to the path and helped him along

it until they could climb onto the gravel road. The boy bent over, panting. Fer rubbed her shoulder, which was sore from him leaning on it.

In the distance, the same dog that had howled before howled again. The boy straightened with a jerk. "Wolves," he muttered.

"No, that's the Carsons' dog," Fer said. She took his arm over her shoulder again. "Come on. It's not very far from here. Grand-Jane is there."

"Why is she grand?" the boy asked.

"It's her name," Fer answered. "She's my *grand*mother, and her name is Jane." Fer had lived with Grand-Jane always, since she was a baby and her parents, Grand-Jane had told her, had "gone from this world," which Fer had always assumed was a nice way of saying that they were dead. She had tried asking her grandma about her parents—how they had died, what they'd been like— but these questions just made Grand-Jane even more quiet . . . as if talking about them made her heart hurt. So Fer didn't ask anymore.

Her grandma wasn't going to like Fer bringing home this strange boy and his wolf bites, not after Fer had run off into the night. Because of that, Grand-Jane would be full of sharp questions and boring punishments.

But Fer couldn't exactly leave an injured person bleeding to death in the bushes, could she?

After what seemed like a long time, they came to the driveway that led to Fer's house. "What's your name?" she asked the boy.

He didn't answer.

Ahead was the house, the windows blazing with light. On the front porch stood a dark figure, the porch light bright behind her.

"Wait here," Fer whispered, and, leaving the boy, squelched across the rain-damp grass to the porch.

Grand-Jane came down the steps, her mouth open to scold. When she saw Fer she stopped.

Silently Fer flung herself at her grandma, a quick, fierce hug, *sorry-for-being-late, sorry-for-making-you-worry.*

Grand-Jane returned the hug, making Fer feel warm and safe, then set her back, arms on her shoulders, looking her over. "You're wet." Her eyes widened and her hands gripped hard with worry. "You're bleeding!"

Fer shook her head. "Not me." She turned and pointed. The boy crouched there, a lump of shadow at the edge of the circle of brightness shed by the porch light. "It's his blood. Wolves bit him."

"*Wolves?*" Grand-Jane asked sharply. She started across the dead, brown grass.

Fer trotted beside her. "Yes, three wolves."

Grand-Jane reached the boy. He looked up.

He had yellow eyes, Fer saw. Gleaming in the light,

like they had little flames burning inside them.

Grand-Jane stared at him. Fer stepped past her and took the boy's arm, helping him to his feet. "Come inside," she said.

"No." Grand-Jane held up her hand. "His kind is not welcome here."

The boy blinked. His yellow eyes narrowed, and he snarled like a dog at Grand-Jane.

Fer looked from Grand-Jane to the boy and back. "What do you mean, his kind? He's hurt."

Grand-Jane shook her head and folded her arms. In the darkness she looked like a stern column. Drops of drizzle shone in her gray hair like diamonds. "We can't help him."

"We're not leaving him out here," Fer said. This was going to be like all of their arguments, wasn't it. Fer protesting, her grandma like a brick wall, unmovable. "He's bleeding. And I said I would help him. I promised."

Grand-Jane didn't answer, but Fer saw a shadow cross her face. After a long moment, she spoke. "You are bound by that promise then, my girl," she said slowly. "Bring him inside."

The boy sagged against Fer. "Come on," she said to him. She dragged him past her grandmother to the porch and up the stairs. Grand-Jane followed. They brought the boy to the warm red-and-yellow kitchen.

"Put him there," Grand-Jane said, pointing at the braided rug next to the table.

Fer lowered the boy to the rug, kneeling beside him. His eyes were closed. His face was pale, except for a smear of blood across his cheek.

Clatter-crash, and Grand-Jane slammed the kettle onto the stove and lit the gas, boiling water. She leaned over and picked a few leaves off the comfrey plant growing in one of the pots along the windowsill. "Get the shirt off him, Jennifer." She stepped out of the kitchen into the stillroom. She'd use herbs to make a poultice, and maybe tea for the pain and to protect against infection.

The boy's eyes flickered open.

"Can you sit up so I can get this off?" Fer asked.

"I'll do it myself," he said. Slowly he sat up, then pulled off the shirt over his head.

She gulped. Two vicious slashes over his ribs, bleeding freshly now that the shirt was pulled away. On his upper arm, deep punctures welling blood, another bite on his shoulder. On his other arm, two deep slashes.

The boy pulled the shirtsleeve away from the bites, wincing. The cloth was clotted with blood.

Fer took the damp shirt from him. Something was pinned to the sleeve. She turned it toward the light to see better. A gleaming black feather, smudged with blood.

"What did she mean, *your kind*?" Fer whispered.

The boy's eyes narrowed. "None of your business."

"It is too my business," Fer said more loudly. "I helped you fight those wolves. I saved you."

Grand-Jane stood in the kitchen doorway, her hands full of bottles and bags of herbs. "You saved his life, Jennifer?" she asked. Her gaze shifted to the boy. "Is that how it is? You owe her your life?"

He looked away.

"*Is* it?" Grand-Jane asked. She crossed to the table and set down the herbs.

He shrugged, then winced. "So what if it is?"

Grand-Jane gave a grim smile. "I may not have much power, but I do have knowledge. I know what you are, Puck," she said. "And I know the rule that binds you." She pointed at the boy. "She saved your life. Now you must swear an oath to repay her."

The boy didn't answer, just glared at Grand-Jane with his yellow eyes.

"Swear the oath!" Grand-Jane said.

Fer shivered, hearing the power in her grandma's voice. She didn't understand what these two were talking about. It was like they knew something she didn't—something old and dangerous.

"I won't," the boy snarled. He turned to Fer. His eyes looked straight into hers—wild eyes, wilder than the wolves or the shadowy black night. He opened his mouth to snap at her and then his eyes widened, as if he'd just realized something. "I can see," he whispered so only Fer could hear. "I know who you are."

"I know who I am too," Fer whispered back. At least, she thought she did. "I want to know who *you* are." She leaned closer. "Wolves were after you, but we don't have wolves here. You didn't tell me your name. Where did you come from? What kind of person are you?"

The boy shook his head, as if shaking off her questions. "You must come back with me," he whispered urgently. "You're the only one who can—" He broke off as Grand-Jane leaned down, putting herself between Fer and the boy.

"Enough," Grand-Jane ordered. "I will put a poultice on those wolf bites, Puck, but then you must go back where you came from and trouble us no more."

The boy looked up at Grand-Jane, and for just a moment he looked like a boy, still shaky from the wolves' attack, frightened, and angry. Very angry.

But when Fer blinked and turned her head slightly away, she saw, out of the corner of her eye, something else, something dangerous and wild, something tricky and not to be trusted.

Something not a boy at all.

❅ ❅ ❅

Rook felt a snarl building in his chest. He wanted to take the shifter-bone from his pocket, pop it into his mouth, and feel it settle under his tongue. He would shift into a horse and trample the sharp-eyed witch and steal away this strange girl who didn't belong on this side of the Way, and then flee on bloody hooves into the night.

If he were a wildling, he would do that. But he wasn't. He wouldn't swear an oath, but the girl *had* saved his life, and even a puck had to admit that he owed her . . . something.

Growling, he picked up his bloody shirt and climbed shakily to his feet. Now that the girl had opened the Way, it would stay open until she closed it. He could go back through. Even with the Mór and her wolves after him, he was better off there than in this strange place. He'd heard his kind couldn't live in this world for long, and now he realized why. This land had no magic. It was ordinary as bread.

The girl knelt on the braided rug, staring at him with wide, gray-blue eyes. She had opened the Way, but he doubted she knew what she had done. He knew who she was, though, knew why the old woman was hiding her here. But he could see clearly enough that the girl was too young and ignorant, and she couldn't do anything to help.

Carefully he pulled the shirt on over his head.

The old grand-woman had backed up a step. She was

afraid of him. Good. She should be.

"The Way is open," he said. He meant it as a warning.

The old woman blinked, and then scowled. "You must close it again."

He shrugged, feeling the sharp ache of the wolf bites. "I can't." He nodded at the girl, still kneeling on the rug. "It opened for her, not for me," he said. "You know as well as I do what she is."

The old woman's face went very pale, and she drew herself up. "She is my granddaughter, and that is all. Now leave here, Puck," she commanded, pointing toward the door. "Go!" she said again. And a third time, she shouted, "Be gone!"

An order given three times had power, even here. He didn't have any choice about it. He went.

three

Fer was brimming with questions, but after the boy left, Grand-Jane slumped into a chair at the kitchen table. "I can't talk about this now, Jennifer," she said, rubbing her eyes as if very tired. She pointed at the stairs. "Go to bed."

Fer went, but she lay in bed for a long time, wondering about the strange boy. *Puck*, her grandma had called him. Grand-Jane had seemed strong and powerful in the kitchen with the boy. And she knew things. Magical things.

During the night Fer sank into the soft darkness of sleep and dreamed of the pool, glimmering with the moon's light. Only this time, it wasn't snarling wolves and a surly boy that came through, shattering the water, it was a woman who came through without a ripple, stepping onto the soft moss. The woman looked young, not much more than a girl, and wore green leggings and a long coat, and knee-high leather boots; her hair was the color of moonlight, and she glowed even more brightly than the moon.

Fer gasped at the young woman's beauty and woke herself up.

"That was a strange dream," she whispered to herself, and her voice sounded papery and thin in the velvety darkness.

The next morning, Grand-Jane stood at the back door with her hands on her hips, surveying the empty fields that stretched to the horizon. A dusting of frost silvered the dirt, and heavy gray clouds covered the sky. Cold air blew in the open door.

"Below freezing last night," Grand-Jane said, frowning. "It's late for that. We won't plant the lettuce today after all."

Fer stepped up beside her, sniffing the cold breeze. She wrinkled her nose. It didn't smell right. Didn't smell like spring coming, as it had the day before. She rubbed at the goose bumps on her arms. "Grand-Jane—" she started to ask, all of her questions piling up in the back of her throat.

"Not now," her grandma snapped back. "I have to think."

Fer swallowed down her questions—for now—and

followed Grand-Jane to the stillroom, where her grandma collected herbs and started grinding them in a mortar. "We never should have let him in." Her hands busy, Grand-Jane nodded toward the kitchen. "Get the honey."

"Why not?" Fer asked. She ducked into the kitchen and grabbed the pot of honey from the table. Bringing it back, she set it on the counter. "Where did the boy go? Do you think he's all right?"

"Oh, that one will always be all right," Grand-Jane said. "Mugwort," she said. "On the top shelf."

Mugwort. That was for protection, and to ward a place from danger. Was the puck-boy dangerous? And the honey, from Grand-Jane's own bees. Fer knew from her lessons on healing lore and magic that the honey would bind the protection to this place even more strongly.

Her grandma reached for a stoppered vial on the shelf over her head. Then she took another mortar and pestle and shoved it down the length of the counter to Fer. "Honey and pennyroyal," she said. "And a pinch of rue. Until it's a fine paste."

Fer gritted her teeth. Fine. If Grand-Jane didn't want to answer questions, Fer knew well enough that there was no point in asking. Not now, at least. Fer pulled the step stool to the counter and climbed up. On the stool she was as tall as her grandma and could bear down on grinding the herbs. She set the mortar on the counter in front of her and poured in a dollop of honey, then added a heap of pennyroyal and a pinch of rue, and set to work. Honey was impossible. She blended herbs and honey until her elbow ached.

After Fer had finished with the herbs and honey, Grand-Jane put her to work dusting the stillroom, from the shelves over the workbench to the boxes of beeswax candles, to the rows of distilling jars that lined the window at the end of the room. While she did that, her grandma took the herb mixture and marked the threshold of the front door and the kitchen door, and every window in the house, while muttering spells under her breath.

"What does it protect against?" Fer asked, coming into the kitchen with an armful of dirty bottles and the sticky mortar and pestle. Grand-Jane stood on a chair smudging a finger-smear of paste along the top edge of the kitchen window.

Grand-Jane dabbed the herb spell into the corners of the window frame. "Against uninvited visitors," she answered.

On Sunday, Grand-Jane sat Fer at the kitchen table. "Where I can keep an eye on you," she said. She plunked down Hildegard's *Causae et Curae* in front of her. "The section on vulnerary herbs." She tapped the book with her finger. "All the way through. Read it aloud."

"I'm going outside after," Fer said. Even though it was pouring down rain, the day pulled at her, the wind whooping around the corners of the house. She didn't care if she got wet out there.

"No, you are not," Grand-Jane said firmly.

While Fer slogged through the reading, Grand-Jane sat across from her at the table, reading glasses perched on her nose, stitching up the tears in Fer's patch-jacket, the ones left by the brambles around the round moon-pool.

Fer paused in her reading. The questions finally overflowed. "The puck-boy said the way is open," she said. "What did he mean by that? What *way* is he talking about? Grand-Jane, what is going on?"

"Never mind. Go on with your reading," Grand-Jane said, and gave Fer a look over the top of her glasses.

"No," Fer said, slapping the book closed. She knew something had happened yesterday, something full of wild magic. And that something had to do with her, and maybe with that strange dream about the lovely woman coming through the moon-pool.

Grand-Jane's mouth set in a straight line. "Then go to your room until you can behave appropriately."

Fer jumped to her feet. For a moment she balanced there, half willing to obey, half ready to flee outside.

If Grand-Jane wasn't going to tell her anything, maybe she could explore the way, find out by herself what her grandmother and the boy were talking about. She took a step toward the door.

"Stop!" Grand-Jane pushed back her chair. "It's too—"

"—*Dangerous*," Fer finished for her. "Why, Grand-Jane? I'm only going outside. Why won't you answer my questions? What are you so afraid of?"

Her grandma paused for a long minute, gazing at Fer. Deciding. "All right." She set her mending on the table and leaned forward in her chair. "Listen, my girl," she said. "Did you think about where that puck came from?"

"I don't even know what a puck *is*." Fer clenched her fists. She would get answers. She *would*. "I know that the boy came from a place where they have wolves. That means he didn't come from anywhere around here. And it looked like he came right through the pool. What is 'the way,' Grand-Jane? And what is a puck?"

Grand-Jane fixed Fer with a sharp eye. "I can see I have no choice. I'd better tell you. Maybe it will make you less likely to go off and get into trouble." She reached out and tapped the closed herbology book. "You know that spells and herbs have power, Jennifer."

Outside, a fierce gust of wind slammed into the house, rattling the windows in their frames. Fer shivered and nodded. Yes, she knew her grandma's magic with the herbs and her bees was real.

"We live here, my girl, because it is close to the Way, and echoes of its magic are felt here, in our world. The Way is—" Grand-Jane shook her head. "It is hard to explain," she muttered to herself. "The Way is like a . . . like a road or a path to get to another place, another land, where the people are very different from us and are governed by different rules. Magic runs through them and their world."

Fer's heart beat faster. This was so much more than just herbs-and-honey magic. "Another . . . place?"

"Yes," Grand-Jane said. "The Way has been closed for a long time. It is supposed to stay closed. It shouldn't . . ." She glanced out the window, where rain was lashing down and the bushes beside the beehives were thrashing in the wild wind. "Maybe it will be all right," she added in a low voice. She stood and started for the still-room.

Fer followed, determined to get the rest. "You still haven't told me what a puck is," she reminded.

"Oh, the puck." Grand-Jane waved her hand, as if waving away a pesky fly. "Pucks are untrustworthy, and they are trouble. That puck didn't like coming through the Way. You'll never see him again."

The puck-boy had been a little frightening, but for some reason Grand-Jane's certainty that he was gone from her life forever made Fer feel a little cold and empty inside.

In the stillroom, Grand-Jane climbed on the step stool and reached onto a high shelf, pushing aside cobwebby bottles. She pulled down a small box and brushed dust from it, then held it out to Fer. "Here."

The box was made of light-colored wood and had the name OWEN carved into the lid. Owen. Her father's name.

"You asked me why I am always afraid for you. I have to keep you safe, Jennifer. Your father went through the Way," Grand-Jane said quietly. "And he never came back."

Fer grabbed the box from her grandma's hands and raced up to her bedroom so she could have a good look at it without Grand-Jane hovering over her like a storm cloud.

Grand-Jane had painted the sloped ceiling in Fer's room blue, like the sky, and she'd painted the walls green, like the cornfields that surrounded the house. Yellow curtains hung over the window at the end of the room, framing the gray sky outside and the rain streaming down the windowpanes. The bed was covered with a quilt made of patches, just like Fer's jacket. Grand-Jane had stitched herbs into the patches and had embroidered

31

spells along the edges of the quilt. It smelled like dusty lavender. It smelled like home, and like safety and protection.

Protection from the Way, Fer was starting to realize, and maybe from the people on the other side . . . in the other place. The Way was real, and the puck-boy had come through it, and maybe the lovely woman from her dream had come through, and her own father had gone through it, gone away forever.

Fer sat on the bed, lifted the hinged lid of the OWEN box, and picked out the contents one by one.

A blurry photograph. On the back, written in smudged blue ink, was the word *Owen*. Fer had never seen a picture of her father before. He was tall, lanky, honey-haired, and not very old. In the picture he stared squint-eyed at the person holding the camera and looked like he was about to open his mouth to speak. What did his voice sound like? And what would he tell her, if he could?

Fer pulled the next thing out of the box. A cloth bag of musty herbs that her nose couldn't identify. The herbs were old and probably didn't have any protective magic left in them.

A black feather. Fer frowned. It was just like the one pinned to the puck-boy's bloody sleeve. The feather should have been dusty and bedraggled, jumbled up in the box as it was, but it shone glossy and bright against the patchwork bedspread. Fer smoothed it with her finger, then set it aside.

The next thing was a flat, round, gray stone about the size of a silver dollar, with a hole in the middle. She held the stone up to her eye to look through it. Blue ceiling, green walls, yellow curtains. Her room, ordinary.

At the bottom of the box was a folded piece of paper, yellowed with age. Scrawled on it in black ink was writing. A letter from Owen, Fer realized. A letter to Grand-Jane from her son.

Mom—

I'll try to explain. You know I never belonged there. I feel right when I am with Laurelin, like I am in the right place for the first time ever in my life. Being with her is like being tangled up in a net of love, and I can't get free even if I wanted to. She is more beautiful and more wonderful than you could ever imagine, even without the glamorie, even though she's a girl, too, just like any girl. Now she is threatened, and so is the land, and I have to help her, because I can't come back to living there like I did before.

Fer looked up from the page. A girl? Like the one from her dream? She read on.

She will close the Way after I go back, and you wouldn't find me anyway, so don't try to come through. Take care of our baby for a little while and I swear an oath to you that I will

33

come back for her as soon as I can, once we have settled this and it's safe. The baby has as much of the others in her as human, so she'll be even more out of place there than I was, and she won't be happy. She'll need to grow up here. You know this, Mom. You know the rules of this land. I bound myself to Laurelin. I have to stand by the oaths I made. The horse is waiting for me, so I have to go back now. If I don't come back, it means we failed. Keep our daughter safe then.

I love you.

Owen

Fer finished reading the letter. Then she read it again.

Owen talked in the letter about *her*. Laurelin, who lived in the other land, the place through the Way. A young woman who was *beautiful* and *wonderful*. The woman Fer had seen in her dream, she felt sure.

And a baby. Owen had asked Grand-Jane to take care of *our baby*. The baby had to be herself. And that meant . . .

"I came from the other place," she whispered. "And my mother was one of them." Outside, thunder grumbled and hail spattered against the windowpanes. Fer shivered.

She blinked and read the letter again. *I swear to you that I will come back for her as soon as I can, once we have settled this and it's safe,* her father had written. But he never had

34

come back, even though he'd promised. Gone away forever, Grand-Jane had said. It still meant *dead*.

Fer had never missed having parents because she'd never known anything different. They'd just been gone. They must have been killed by something or someone on the other side of the Way. No wonder Grand-Jane had refused to talk about them.

But now she knew. She knew about her parents, and she knew she was from somewhere else, far away.

And it wasn't like being from Finland or Japan, either, but from a place of magic and danger and people that, maybe, weren't really people at all. She'd told the puck-boy that she knew who she was, but now she didn't.

She had no idea at all.

four

When Rook went back through the Way, the Mór was waiting for him, standing on the mossy bank with her three wolf-guards looming up behind her, no longer in their wolf shapes, but people. One of the Mór's crows perched on her shoulder. The full moon shone down, filling the clearing with bright light and sharp, black shadows. The air was icy cold.

Rook crouched at the Mór's feet, his head lowered. He'd tried to get away, but she'd called the hunt down on him. Now he was at her mercy.

And the Mór was not known for being merciful.

"That Way has been closed for a long time," the Mór said mildly.

Rook looked up. She didn't sound angry.

In the moonlight her glamorie surrounded her like a glowing aura, making her look young and strong and dangerously beautiful. Her short black hair gleamed like a crow's wing; her eyes were deep and filled with stars, like a winter sky at night. Rook caught his breath and blinked, trying to see through the glamorie to the real Mór.

"And yet now the Way is open," she said.

So it was. Rook stole a quick glance over his shoulder. The water of the pool rippled under the silver moonlight. The girl was the one who'd opened it. But the Mór didn't need to know about her; the girl would be safer if she didn't.

"Yet you went through," the Mór said. "What did you find on the other side?"

Rook shrugged, and he felt the burning ache of the wolf bites on his arms and chest. He didn't want to tell her.

The Mór frowned. On her shoulder, the crow shifted, watching Rook with a glinting eye. "Always resisting, aren't you, Robin?" She sighed. "So I will make it an order. Tell me what you found."

The rule said that he only had to answer the question as it was asked. "The Mór must be obeyed," he said bitterly.

"I am the Lady now, and that is what you will call me," she ordered. "And you will tell me what you found."

"I found trees, Lady," he said, with a bitter accent on the word *Lady*. "A land on the edge of springtime. Bushes. Rain." He paused. "Lots of mud. Lady."

"You are testing the limits of my patience, Robin," the Mór said, her voice taut. "Let me rephrase the question. *Who* did you find on the other side of the Way?"

Now he had no choice but to answer. "A girl," Rook said sullenly. "A girl named"—What had the grandmother called her? A strange name—"Jennifer."

"Ah," the Mór breathed. "Not Jennifer. *Gwynnefar*. At last. Very well done indeed, my clever puck." She leaned down and took his arm, jerking him to his feet. Rook blinked the glamorie away and saw the true Mór behind it, bent and sunken-eyed and thin, with dull, black hair. He shuddered.

Her sharp eyes noted his reaction as his puck vision saw through her glamorie. Then she took in the darker patches of blood on his torn shirt. Her clawlike hand gripped his arm tightly, right where her wolves' teeth had bitten the deepest. "You have been punished enough, I think, Robin. Your wounds will be treated, and then I will tell you how you will serve your Lady next."

※ ※ ※

Fer tried asking Grand-Jane all the questions the letter had left her with. But Grand-Jane got quieter and more stern and finally snapped. "You read the letter, didn't you, Jennifer?" When Fer nodded, Grand-Jane went on. "That means you know as much as I do."

"But how did they meet, if she was from the other side of the Way?" Fer asked.

With a sigh, Grand-Jane told Fer a little more. Owen had been a wanderer, she said, the way Fer was, and one twilit evening he'd stumbled onto the Way. The moon had shone down and the Way had opened, and a beautiful girl had stepped out.

Fer could imagine it, like a picture from a story. The round moon-pool, her tall, sandy-haired father falling in love with the moonlit woman from the other place.

Grand-Jane seemed to know what she was thinking. "Don't fool yourself, Jennifer," Grand-Jane said. "She bewitched Owen. I don't know how it happened, but somehow she died, and she drew Owen to his death."

"But he loved her!" Fer protested. There was a whole story here, one she needed to hear. It couldn't end with death, could it?

"Oh, I don't know." Grand-Jane rubbed her eyes, as if weary. "The point is that in the letter, Owen swore an oath to return for you. He didn't come back, so it is clear that he is dead, and so is she. Something happened there that killed them both and there is nothing more to be done about it. You know enough now. Just keep away from the Way, and stop asking questions. Please, Jennifer!"

So Fer stopped asking. The chilly house on Sunday felt full of silence, full of old hurts and new fears because Fer could tell that Grand-Jane was afraid. She'd never known her fierce grandma to fear anything.

But the more she thought about it, the more sure she was that Grand-Jane was wrong. There was more to this story. More that Grand-Jane didn't know and didn't want to know. Owen really *had* loved Laurelin; he hadn't just been bewitched by her. And—his letter hadn't said so—but Laurelin had loved him, too, hadn't she? Grand-Jane didn't want to know the real ending to their story. She liked silence better.

By Monday, Fer was grateful for school, even though school was awful. Just to get out of the house, without Grand-Jane's grim silence and without her keen eyes *watching* her all the time! Did Grand-Jane think *she* was dangerous, like the puck-boy? Or like she seemed to think Fer's mother had been? Maybe she was dangerous, if she was one of them, as her father's letter had said. She didn't feel dangerous. . . .

She wasn't sure what she felt. Lost, maybe. Like she couldn't feel the ground under her feet, like she didn't know what was real anymore, and what was not.

Outside, a cold rain drizzled down. Fer put on her raincoat and rubber boots and slung on her backpack.

Grand-Jane wouldn't let her walk to the bus stop

alone today. She came too, under a black umbrella. The bare branches of the oak trees were slick and black with rainwater, the driveway muddy. Fer kicked through the puddles and stood shivering with her grandma at the corner, where the driveway met the gravel road.

Grand-Jane frowned. "I don't like the looks of this weather."

Fer stayed quiet.

"And I don't like the feel of it," Grand-Jane muttered.

Now that she thought about it, the weather didn't feel right to Fer, either. She couldn't feel, as she had before, the spring ready to burst forth, full of life and birdsong and bright sunshine. Everything felt dead, and too quiet. The land stretched out flat around them, straight roads leading to other straight roads, leading to town, laid out in its careful grid. Fer looked over the muddy fields. In the distance, a smudge on the flat line of the horizon was the Carsons' dairy farm, the gray silos and outbuildings almost lost in the downpour. Past that was the wooded ravine where the stream wound across the square field.

Maybe after school today . . .

"I'll be here to meet you this afternoon, Jennifer," Grand-Jane said, as the bus pulled up in a spray of gravel. The doors creaked open.

"Why don't you just put a leash on me, if you're so

afraid?" Fer said, not quite loud enough for Grand-Jane to hear. Then she climbed onto the bus.

Fer never felt like an oddball until she got on the bus or arrived at school with the other kids. The normal ones, with ordinary families. She didn't really want to be like them, but they wanted her to be like them. The *Jenny-furhead* thing was bad enough, but even worse was the hairy eyeball they gave her whenever she did something that reminded them of how different she really was.

Part of the problem was the bees. When she'd been in kindergarten, her class had sat outside to eat lunch, and the other kids had shrieked and swatted when bees swarmed around them and their sticky peanut-butter-and-jelly sandwiches and purple juice. Fer had set down her tofu and watercress burrito and stood up to use the small magic Grand-Jane had taught her. She'd gathered the bees around her, and then with a flick of a finger sent them zooming in formation around the playground and then off into the blue sky. Fer had done it to help and to be nice, but the other kids didn't think it was nice. They just thought it was weird, and they hadn't forgotten it.

They thought Fer smelled funny, too. Which she did, because of Grand-Jane's herbal spells that she had to carry in her pockets all the time.

And there was something else. Every time Fer stepped

onto the school bus, her head started to ache. She could feel the oily exhaust from the bus settle onto her skin, making her itch. As the bus drove closer to town, farther from the open air of the country, the headache got worse. By the time she stepped out onto the cement sidewalk in front of the school, the tips of her fingers and toes had gone numb, and a gray fog swirled in front of her eyes. She tripped, stumbled; her tongue got twisted and she couldn't quite speak what she meant to say. On a bad day, she got a rash that spread from her hands and up her arms, and then crept up the back of her neck. And the headache . . .

It was always awful like this. She'd tried to explain to Grand-Jane that the bus and school and town felt *wrong* somehow, that it made her sick, but her grandma insisted that she go to school, and Fer was always better by the time she got home.

Now she knew she really *was* different, and it was even worse. She stumbled off the bus, then trudged across the sidewalk and up the steps into the school. A push from behind, and Emily Bradley shoved past with her friend. "The bee girl's not wearing the quilt with sleeves," Emily said scornfully.

Fer blinked. She had something fierce to say about the patchwork jacket Grand-Jane had made her, but as usual the noisy hallway and the fluorescent lights buzzing overhead made the words fly out of her head. She clenched her fists, ready to fight instead.

But today would not be a good day to get into a fight. Fer slouched into her seat in the classroom, feeling slow and stupid and numb.

After an endless day at school, Fer got on the bus for the ride home. Instead of getting off at her stop, where Grand-Jane would be waiting, she got off a stop early with some other kids.

The bus door cranked closed behind Fer and the bus pulled away with a spurt of wet gravel and a smell of oily smoke. Fer waited until the silence had settled around her. The headache and dullness of asphalt and fluorescent lights and chain-link fences and linoleum slowly drained away. She took a deep breath. The sky stretched wide and gray overhead; the fields stretched muddy and cold to either side. Rain pattered down. Spring would come soon, and the farmers would start their planting, but now the fields looked brown and dead. Fer closed her eyes, frowning. They *felt* brown and dead too, as if something was missing, or wrong.

Fer headed down the road until she got to the place where the culvert let the stream pass under the road. She scrambled down. The stream bubbled and boiled, full of the day's rain. Blinking raindrops out of her eyes, Fer headed downstream, toward the round moon-pool.

Toward the Way. Grand-Jane's spells and honey and herbs were magic, but it was homey magic, comfortable magic. It had nothing to do with a black dog that turned into a boy with yellow eyes. Or with snarling wolves. Or with a crescent moon in the sky that reflected full and fat in a perfectly round pool. Those things were *real* magic.

Crawk!

Fer looked up. On a dead branch over her head perched a black crow. It cocked its head, examining her with a sharp, silver eye. *Crawk!* it said again. Then it dropped from its perch and flapped away, heading downstream.

Fer's feet found the path that led along the stream and she followed it, her school backpack heavy, her boots crusted with mud. She looked up to see more crows. They perched in the trees, silent. Watching.

She went on. The crows followed, flapping from perch to perch. The path ended, and Fer pushed through a clump of dripping bushes and brambles, and stepped out onto the bank of the moon-pool. Rainwater had filled it to overflowing; the moss around its edges was sodden. Falling rain hissed on the surface of the water.

It looked like an ordinary pool of water, not a magical Way. Fer peered through the rain and saw three gray shapes on the other side of the pool. Like wisps of fog, the shapes floated around the pool toward her. She saw fur, bushy tails, gleaming eyes.

The wolves!

Fer groped in the pocket of her raincoat. No spell-bag of herbs—she'd left it in her patch-jacket pocket. And no heavy branch to swing at them, either.

The wolves paced toward her, growling.

Fer stepped back, ready to run, when something else emerged from the mist, dark and person-shaped. It was the puck-boy. He spoke sharply to the wolves, and they faded back to the edge of the forest and lurked there in the mist.

The puck-boy looked different from the last time she'd seen him. Before, he'd been ragged and sort of desperate and frightened. Coming around the edge of the pool to where she waited, he looked stiff and formal, wearing a black woolen coat a little like a uniform, with a black feather pinned to the sleeve.

"Hi," she said. "Are you all right?"

He stared blankly at her. "What?"

"The wolf bites. Did you get them taken care of?"

"Oh." He frowned. "I did, yes."

In the trees all around, the crows sat silent. That was a strange way for birds to behave. Their watching silver eyes made Fer's skin feel prickly.

The wolves were watching too. One of them circled the pool, flowing like quicksilver over a dead log and around a tree. It yipped and another yipped back an answer—as if they were talking to each other.

Keeping an eye on them, Fer spoke to the puck-boy. "Are those wolves going to attack us?"

He didn't even glance aside at them. "They are not. They're under orders."

"Whose orders?" Fer asked.

"I am sent to bring you through the Way," the puck-boy said, ignoring her question. "The Lady invites you to come."

Fer's heart jumped in her chest. "The Lady?" she asked. "Who is that?"

"She is the . . ." He hesitated, then went on. "She is a Lady of that place. She wants to meet you."

"I know that my father went to be with my mother on the other side of the Way," Fer said. "Is that why the Lady wants me to come? Did she know them? Does she know what happened to them?"

"The Lady will answer your questions," the puck-boy said again, his voice flat.

Fer felt a flare of excitement. That's what she wanted— answers to her questions. Like who she really was and what had happened to her parents. "I want to come through the Way," she said.

"Then come." He held out a hand.

Fer took a step toward him, then stopped. Wait. What

about Grand-Jane? She couldn't just disappear the way her father had. "I can't." She gave a frustrated sigh. "I have to go back and tell my grandma."

"She'll not let you come," the puck-boy said.

He was right about that. But one way or another, Fer would get through the Way. "Just wait," she told him. "I'll be back as soon as I can."

five

Fer ran all the way home. Grand-Jane was going to be so mad about her getting off the bus early and going to the moon-pool. Grand-Jane could shout all she wanted, but Fer was going through the Way. Maybe she could find out how, exactly, her father and mother had died. And she could learn from the Lady who she really was, what it meant to have a mother who had lived in that other land. Fer thought about her father's hastily scribbled note. *You know I never belonged there*, he'd written. *And I feel right when I am with Laurelin, like I am in the right place for the first time ever in my life.*

Fer knew what it was like to feel, like an itch under her skin or a faint ache behind her eyes, that she was wrong. The wrong person in the wrong place. She felt a rush of warmth for her father, even though she'd never known him. He had been just like her. Maybe, through the Way, it would be different.

Fer ran *crunch-splash-crunch* through the puddles on the driveway. Crows had gathered in the branches of the oak trees and cawed at her as she went past. Ignoring them, Fer ran around to the back of the house, went up the stairs, and burst into the kitchen.

Grand-Jane came out of the stillroom, wiping her hands on a rag. Without speaking, she leaned against the stillroom doorway, her eyes narrowed. Fer knew that look. Grand-Jane was furious.

Fer caught her breath and rubbed the raindrops off her face with the back of her hand. She took a step farther into the kitchen.

"Boots," Grand-Jane said sharply.

Fer bent over and slipped the muddy boots off her feet, then straightened. Might as well get it over with. "I went to the Way."

Grand-Jane froze.

"I met the puck-boy again," Fer said. "He asked me to come to the other place. I'm going."

Grand-Jane caught her breath and clenched her hands around the dirty rag. "You will *not* go," she said fiercely.

Fer gulped. Now that she actually had to *tell* Grand-Jane, it wasn't so simple. A lump rose up in her throat, blocking her voice.

"I will not lose you, my girl," Grand-Jane said.

The way she'd lost Owen, she meant. Fer tried another argument. "The puck-boy says a Lady wants to see me. I'm invited."

Grand-Jane didn't speak.

"I—" Fer started. Maybe this would work. "What if I promise to come back? Will you let me go then?"

When Grand-Jane spoke, her usually sharp voice was a despairing croak. "Whether I let you go or not, you'll go anyway, just as Owen did."

"I have to go. I *have* to," Fer said. Grand-Jane could watch and protect and guard, just as she'd always done, but somehow Fer would get through the Way.

A sigh shuddered out of Grand-Jane. "All right." She shook her head, and that seemed to shake her out of her frozen despair. "All right," she repeated more steadily. She set the rag on the counter with shaking hands. "I can see I have no choice. Say it."

Fer blinked. "Say what?"

"Your oath," Grand-Jane said impatiently.

All right. "I promise to come back."

"This is not just a promise, Jennifer. It's an oath. You are bound by that oath," Grand-Jane said.

"I'm not sure what that means, Grand-Jane," she said shakily.

Grand-Jane's eyes narrowed. "You will have to learn the rules that govern the people through the Way. It is not the same as here. Now, we will pack some things and I will tell you as much as I know. I won't let you go there unprotected."

The night was velvety dark. Her backpack weighing on her shoulders, Fer padded up the path toward the pool. A breeze rustled through the bare branches of the trees, and off to her left the stream gurgled. The rain had stopped and a chilly wind had blown the heavy clouds away. Overhead the crescent moon gave Fer enough light to see the path snaking along before her.

As she came up to the pool, Fer slowed to a walk. Her sneakered feet were silent on the mossy bank. She felt jittery with excitement. The pool's water was ruffled by the breeze, making the reflection of the moon wavery. It wasn't a full moon reflected in the water, but the crescent moon.

No puck-boy was waiting for her.

Fer slung the backpack onto the damp ground and sat down next to the pool. He would come for her, and when he did, she'd be ready.

Fer wore sneakers and jeans, a warm sweater, and over it, her patch-jacket. A spell-bag of protective herbs was in her pocket. Her backpack was stuffed with a change of clothes, a nightgown, a toothbrush and toothpaste, and, nestled at the bottom, the wooden box with OWEN on the lid. Grand-Jane had added bags of healing herbs and vials of tincture to the box and insisted she take it with her.

While Grand-Jane had packed the clothes into Fer's backpack, Fer hadn't been able to sit still; she'd pulled clothes out of her dresser drawers and piled them on the bed.

"Listen, my girl," Grand-Jane had said. "I've lived close to the Way for my entire life, and I've seen things and read things that you need to know. In that land, swearing an oath is more than just making a promise. If you swear an oath to do something, you *must* do it, or terrible things will happen. If their land is like cloth, then a broken oath is like a stain on that cloth, a stain that will never come out. Do you understand?"

Fer nodded. She understood. Oaths were bone deep, and broken oaths broke the land, too.

"Good," Grand-Jane said. "Now, did you notice that I ordered the puck three times to leave our house?"

Grand-Jane had seemed very powerful in that moment. Fer nodded again.

"Mmm," Grand-Jane said, and looked at Fer with pursed lips. "Another rule of their kind is the rule of three. An order given three times requires obedience. An oath of loyalty given three times binds the swearer absolutely, until death. A question asked three times has power; it compels the one asked to answer. But it's not a power to be used lightly, not with their kind, because

53

you never know, with them, how your questions might bind you. You must be very, very careful who you ask, and what questions you ask them."

"What do you mean by their 'kind'?" Fer asked. "You said they're not human. What are they?" And what was she, exactly?

"They are wilder than we are, and have animal or plant . . ." She paused. "Not spirits, exactly. It's as if they evolved to become what they now are from different animals, like foxes and deer and eagles. Or from trees, like birches or pines. They were those things at one time, and are still tied to them. Some part of them remains a fox, or a deer, or a tree. It is a kind of magic we do not have here."

"So the puck-boy is really a dog?" Fer asked.

"No, the puck is something else altogether. Pucks are loyal to no one and serve no one, except in very rare situations. That's why he wouldn't swear an oath to you, Jennifer, even after you saved his life. Pucks have many names and can change shape, which is why you saw him as a dog first. They make trouble wherever they go, and they go wherever they will. You must be very careful not to let the puck lead you into danger." Grand-Jane went to Fer's dresser and took out a pair of socks. "Here. Take an extra pair."

Fer took them and wedged them in beside the OWEN

box. "And I'm one of these other people?" she dared ask.

Grand-Jane gave her a curt nod. "There's more of them in you than I realized. It is dangerous for you to go, but I see that we don't have any choice about this." Then Grand-Jane added three more things to Fer's backpack: a bottle with a cork stopper, a pencil, and a tight roll of paper. For writing messages, she said, that Fer could send back through the Way.

"I'm not sending you without protection," Grand-Jane said. "I can't do much from here, but you will have more questions. The Way is open, so I can send you what answers I have, if you need them."

Fer stared at the pool, thinking about oaths that bound. And about why she was going. Grand-Jane was worried and frightened, but she didn't need to be. Fer felt something pulling at her from that other place, something she felt in her bones. Her father had said she belonged there. Maybe she did. And she had a story without an ending pulling at her too.

The water rippled, and then it stilled. The night around her fell silent. She blinked, and the crescent moon reflected in the still pool water grew fat and round and yellow.

Fer climbed to her feet and slung the backpack over her shoulders. The Way was open, the puck-boy had said. He was supposed to meet her. Where was he?

The air grew taut with waiting. "Come *on*," Fer whispered.

Nothing happened. The night was so quiet, Fer heard the sound of her own heart beating. She gazed down at the pool.

When the puck-boy and the wolves had come through the Way, the moon-pool had shattered. But the wolves hadn't been dripping wet. The puck-boy hadn't been wet, either. Just bloody.

Fer rubbed her fingertips together, remembering the tingle of power she'd felt when the wolves and the puck-boy had come through the pool. The Way was open.

Without a second thought, Fer took a deep breath, and jumped.

six

She fell.

Everything went dark. A bitterly cold wind rushed around her. She blew like a leaf, tumbling over and over again. The wind tore the pack off her back and flung it away; her braided hair unraveled and swirled around her head. The heavy smell of cold dirt filled her nose. The wind fell silent. She opened her mouth and reached for a breath and found no air, just emptiness. She floated.

Then a sudden jolt.

Fer gasped in a breath. She sat up and brushed tangled hair out of her eyes. The starry sky whirled overhead, then steadied. She was sprawled on the ground next to the pool, her backpack beside her. The water lapped at the same springy moss; the same tangle of bushes stood like a dark wall behind her and, overhead, bare-branched trees were silhouetted against the moonlight.

It hadn't worked. The Way hadn't taken her through.

Wait. Fer looked up. The fat, golden, round moon had moved up into the sky, and the silver-crescent moon from her world was reflected in the pool. And, she noticed, she wasn't dripping wet. She *had* gone through.

The bushes behind her rustled. "Well, it took you long enough," a rough voice said.

Fer scrambled to her feet. The puck-boy, his face just a pale blur in the darkness. "Hi," she said.

He stepped out of the shadow of the bushes. In the moonlight she could see him better, and he was frowning. "You look glad to see me."

"I *am* glad to see you," Fer said. She really was, despite Grand-Jane's warning about pucks. "I think you should tell me your name now."

"What does that have to do with anything?" the puck-boy said.

"People should know each others' names," Fer said. These others might have rules, but she had rules too. Like asking if somebody who'd been hurt was okay, and knowing what people called themselves. "You already know my name. It's Jennifer. But it's really Fer."

The puck-boy frowned again. "You gave me yours freely," he muttered, "so I don't have much choice about it, do I?"

"I don't know. Do you?" Fer asked.

"I don't," he growled. "It's Rook."

Rook? What kind of name was Rook? Oh, wait. What had Grand-Jane said about the pucks? "Do you have lots of different names?" Fer asked.

Rook gave her a cagey look. "I'm known by other names in other places. Here I'm Rook. Can we get on with it?"

Fer nodded. "Are you supposed to take me to the Lady?"

Rook gave a stiff shrug. "Yes. And you are late. Hurry up." He turned and headed down a path that looked just like the path Fer had used to come to the pool. Fer picked up her backpack, slung it over her shoulders, and followed.

It had rained here, too, and the path was muddy and it was even colder and more dismal than at home. A brisk wind rattled the bare tree branches and tangled in Fer's hair. She dug in her jeans pocket for an extra rubber band and tied her hair back into a messy ponytail.

Rook didn't talk, just led on through the moon-silvered darkness. In her world they would have come to the gravel road by now, or some farmer's muddy field. Instead the forest grew thicker. Moonlight filtered through the branches, sending sharp-edged shadows across the path. Under Fer's feet the ground felt more . . . solid somehow. The air felt cleaner, clearer. They left the stream, the path leading up a hill and down the other side. Fer's backpack grew heavier, but her steps felt lighter.

They came out of the forest and crossed a meadow rustling with waist-high dry grasses. In the wide, purple-black sky, the moon leaned toward the earth, getting ready to set. The meadow ended and the forest swallowed up the path again.

Fer followed Rook through the waning night. All around her she felt the forest, dark and mysterious. The air felt wound tight, as if it was waiting for something. Fer felt her eyesight growing more keen; it was almost like she could see deep into the sharp slices of shadows between the trees. They'd been walking for what Fer guessed was another hour when Rook stopped suddenly and she bumped into his back. Peering over his shoulder, she saw two dark figures blocking the path. They stepped closer, into a patch of fading moonlight. A man and a woman, both dressed in gray, both with raggedy-rough gray hair and sharp eyes. Guards. The woman turned, and Fer caught a glimpse of a crow feather—the same kind of feather she'd seen on Rook's bloody sleeve back at Grand-Jane's house—pinned to the sleeve of her gray shirt.

"It's the puck!" the man said.

"Imagine that," the woman said. "Hey-ho, Puck!" She grabbed Rook's arm and he flinched. He'd been bitten on that arm, Fer remembered.

Rook jerked his arm out of her grasp and reached back. Fer felt his fingers close over hers; then he tried to push past the man and woman. They blocked him. "What've you got there, puppy-puck?" the man asked, leering down at Fer. Beside him, the woman grinned, her teeth sharp and shining in the moonlight.

Rook was taller than Fer was, and he looked older, like a high school boy. Next to the looming gray-clad guards he seemed slight and young. Ignoring the guard's question, he gripped Fer's hand tightly. She saw him put his other hand into his pocket. He'd done that before, hadn't he? What did he keep in there?

The guards stepped closer, crowding.

"Back off," Rook snarled up into their faces. "I'm under orders."

"So are we," the woman said. "The hunt is on."

Rook dropped Fer's hand. "What, now?" he asked.

Both guards nodded, grinning.

Something about their grins looked familiar. "Have I seen you before?" Fer asked.

The woman turned her leering smile on Fer. "I don't know, girlie. *Have* you?"

Fer tried her trick, the one she'd used to see Rook better when she first met him, turning her head to look out of the corner of her eyes. She caught a quick glimpse of the woman's face warping into a gray muzzle, the wide mouth full of teeth. Tufted gray ears poked up through her hair.

The people of this land had once been wild, Grand-Jane had told her. Now Fer knew it for sure. This wolf-woman had chased Rook through the Way and bit him. Fer put her hand into her jacket pocket and gripped the cloth bag with the protective spell in it. "We're supposed to go to the Lady," she said. "And we're late. You'd better let us go."

The wolf-guard flinched. "Aoooww!" She turned to the other guard. "This girl's got a protective spell on her."

"We should bite her then, right?" the man asked.

"No!" the woman reached out and tweaked his ear. "We should let 'em go." She pulled her partner off the path. "Take the girl to the Lady," she ordered Rook.

"That's what I'm doing," Rook answered with a scowl. He grabbed Fer's arm and shoved her past the wolf-guards, ahead of him down the path. "Stupid wolves," he muttered.

Fer stumbled away from the guards who were really wolves. It was a strange place, where people could be animals and animals could be people.

She kept going on the path, Rook a silent shadow at her back. They walked for a little while, until Rook's hand came down on her shoulder. "Wait," he whispered. "The hunt is coming." In the moonlight, his face was very pale. He stepped around her and led her down the path a little farther. They came out of the forest and into a wide clearing.

The moon, huge and white, hung tangled in the highest branches of the trees on the other side of the clearing, spreading its dying light across the grass. The trees and bushes around the edge were dark shadows. All was quiet. Fer's ears strained at the night.

Then she heard a thrashing of bushes across from them, and an animal crashed into the clearing. A stag, huge, its antlers silvered with moonlight. It stumbled into the middle of the clearing, one heaving flank stained with black—blood. An arrow jutted from the wound. The stag raised its head, panting, listening.

Fer caught her breath. It was so beautiful. . . .

At the sound, the stag's head turned and he stared straight at Fer, and seeing her, he didn't shy away like a deer should have. His gaze was frightened. He wasn't just an animal; he was something else, too. She felt a connection spin itself like a gleaming thread between herself and the stag. She stepped toward him and turned her head, trying to catch a glimpse of what he really was.

She felt Rook's hand on her arm, holding her back.

"He's hurt," Fer whispered. The connection to the stag pulled at her. "We have to help." Maybe she could get the arrow out and stop the bleeding.

"It's too late," Rook said harshly. "The hunt is here."

As he spoke, the quiet night shattered like breaking glass—the sound of horns, trampling hoofbeats, a rushing wind—and a horse leaped into the clearing. Its rider, dressed all in black, jerked an arrow from the quiver on its back, fitted it to a bowstring, and smoothly released it. The arrow, trailing sparks, flashed across the clearing and buried itself in the stag's throat. With a scream, the stag crashed to the ground.

Fer tore her arm from Rook's grasp and raced across the grass to the stag. He lay in a puddle of moonlight, black blood flowing from his mouth. "Oh, no," Fer whispered. She knelt beside the stag. His eye fixed on her, deep as a forest pool.

Before she took her next shaking breath, the stag's eye turned glassy. The thread that connected them snapped, and Fer felt his death as a wrongness that rolled up from the bloodstained grass and into her, making her hands shake and her vision waver. She could feel the stag's hot blood as it seeped into the dirt, deeper and deeper, a black stain that could never be washed away. But the stain had power, too, a kind of black, sparking power that spread outward from the clearing, passing like a shadow over the moon. Fer blinked, shaking her head. The night seemed dimmer, darker than it had before.

Behind her, Fer heard hoofbeats muffled by dried

grass, the jingling of harnesses, and soft whispers. Shaking off the wrongness, she got to her feet, feeling the same fierceness she'd felt when she'd saved Rook from the wolves—ready to find a big stick and bash whoever had killed the stag. A horse and rider loomed over her. The shadows shifted and the moonlight revealed a woman.

Her face reminded Fer of a statue, pale and chiseled out of the finest translucent marble. Her short, black hair was held back with a silver cord. Her eyes shone like stars. She sat straight and slim on the back of a tall black horse that wore no saddle and had a bridle made from a silver chain.

The Lady, Fer realized. The one Rook had brought her here to meet. It had to be. Fer stared up at the Lady and her fierceness melted away. Instead she felt like she'd been caught up in a net, captured by the Lady's beauty and power.

Behind the Lady was a shadowy group of other riders, mounted on tall horses, and on goats or on stags like the one that had been killed. They shifted, the mounts panting, tired from the chase. But they didn't speak.

Gracefully the Lady slipped down from the horse's back, still holding the bow.

Rook had ghosted up and stood just behind Fer. The Lady handed him the horse's silver chain. Rook took it, his face blank. The horse snuffled a greeting into Rook's neck, then rested its nose on his shoulder.

The Lady stepped closer and embraced Fer, then leaned down to kiss her forehead. "Gwynnefar," she said, her voice as silver and bright as the flowing moonlight. "Your mother was my closest ally, and it is right that you have come here. I am the Lady of this place, and I make you most welcome." A single black feather appeared in her hand. "This is for you," the Lady said. "It marks that you are mine."

Fer found herself holding out her hand, and the Lady laid the feather across it.

The Lady smiled and turned Fer to face her retinue. The dead stag lay at their feet. Its blood had soaked into the ground. "This is Gwynnefar," the Lady announced. "Make her most welcome!"

The shadows bowed from atop their mounts.

The Lady grasped her horse's mane and leaped gracefully onto its back. Rook released the bridle. "See that she is well settled," the Lady ordered.

Rook nodded.

Fer stared up at the Lady, who glowed with beauty in the dying moonlight. Her mother had been this Lady's ally. Maybe this was her place, and she would serve this beautiful silver-moonlight Lady too.

seven

"She's so beautiful," Fer said to Rook.

"Oh, she is that," he answered, but Fer thought she heard a hint of scorn in his voice. He led her back to the path, moving awkwardly, as if his wolf bites were hurting. "Come on."

After a few minutes of walking, Fer paused and sniffed. The air didn't smell like the cold nub end of winter. She sniffed again. It smelled of rich, damp dirt. A breeze blew through the tree branches and—did she hear leaves rustling? Alongside the narrow path, ferns crowded in. She crouched. In the moonlight, the ferns were graceful dark curls edged with silver, their smell sharp and green. She touched one and it unfurled under her fingers.

"It's spring," she whispered. Along with the ferns, bloodroot poked from the dead leaves, its flowers closed up tight against the night. And toadshade, and tender wild geranium. Around a rotting tree stump on the other side of the path grew soft moss and tiny toadstools that glowed white under the moon, like buttons. Fer stroked the moss. It felt springy and prickly under her hand. Rook had turned on the path ahead, waiting. "It wasn't spring before," she said, "and now it is. It's like magic."

"It *is* magic," Rook answered, his voice rough against the soft night. "It comes from her. From the Lady."

The Lady had the power to make spring blossom out of winter? How had she done it?

Rook walked away down the trail. As Fer got to her feet, ready to follow him, she heard a rustling behind her. She turned to look and caught a glimpse of a face fading back into the shadows. A broad, old face with a wide mouth and nose and what looked to Fer like leaves for hair, and—Fer stepped closer to see—was her skin green? It was hard to tell in the moonlight.

"Hello?" Fer called softly. She blinked and saw more of the green woman, a short, stocky body that reminded her of a mossy stump sunk into the ground.

The green woman bowed her head, a greeting. "So you are Gwynnefar, are you?" she asked. Her voice was deep, like the sound of a high waterfall crashing onto rocks. "Opened the Way and came through?"

Fer nodded.

"Has spring come to the land on the other side of the

Way?" the green woman asked.

That was a strange question. Fer thought of the oak leaves still in their buds and the bees asleep in their hives. And of the cold, dead feeling of the fields around Grand-Jane's house. "No," she answered. "Spring hasn't come there yet."

"Hmph," the green woman grunted. "Does this spring you see here feel right to you? Tell me, girl!"

Startled, Fer closed her eyes to see if she could sense the land as she had before. Yes, she could feel the land easing away from winter, opening itself to warmth and life. But over it . . .

She frowned. Over it she felt a taint. Like a shadow— one that left her skin prickling with goose bumps. "No. No, it doesn't feel right," Fer said with a shiver. She opened her eyes, but the green woman had disappeared.

Fer heard footsteps on the path.

"We need to go on," Rook said sharply.

"Okay," Fer said. She checked the shadows, but the green woman was really gone. "Did you see her?"

"Who?" Rook said over his shoulder, leading her away.

"That woman," Fer said. "Her hair was made out of leaves."

Rook stopped suddenly and faced her. "Leaf Woman? You saw her?"

"She didn't tell me her name, Rook. She was green, I think," Fer said.

He frowned. "You must be mistaken. Leaf Woman has gone . . ." He shook his head. ". . . away. And she doesn't show herself to strangers." He turned back to the path. "Come on."

Fer followed. "Maybe I'm not a stranger, Rook," she whispered. But he didn't hear her.

❋ ❋ ❋

As the night lifted and pink dawn crept in, Rook led the girl along the trampled path left by the hunt, back toward the wide meadow where the Lady's retinue was encamped. The girl stumbled with weariness, yet looked around with wide, curious eyes.

She *had* been glad to see him when they'd met at the Way. Why? She must want something from him, Rook figured. At some awkward moment she'd remind him that she'd saved his life, and then there would be trouble. For her, he hoped, and not for himself.

She stepped up beside him. "The Lady called me Gwynnefar. Is that my name in this place?"

"It is," Rook answered.

"She's so beautiful," she said musingly. She rubbed at the spot on her forehead where the Lady had kissed her.

He didn't answer. He could see she was still affected by the Mór's glamorie, the magic the Mór had stolen from the true Lady of the land; the magic she surrounded herself with to hide what she truly was.

They stepped out of the forest. Under their feet, the grass was wet with dew. Across the wide meadow, tents were arrayed, billowing silk tinged pink by the dawn light. Rook stopped and pointed. "That tent in the middle, the big white one, is for the Lady." The other, smaller tents were sky blue and the darker blue-green of the sky just after sunset, and grass-green, and fern-green, and the purple of the violets that grew on the forest floor. "The blue tent at the edge there—" He pointed. "That'll be for you."

"It looks fine," she said. "Rook, my father's name was Owen and he came here a long time ago to be with my mother, whose name was Laurelin. Grand-Jane thinks they're both dead. Did you know them?"

Rook was silent. It hadn't been that long ago. It had all happened just before he'd joined the Mór's retinue, when he'd bound himself to her to redeem his puck-brother's oath. A few turnings of the seasons here, that was all. Longer in the girl's world. Owen, her father, was dead; he knew that much, and Laurelin with him. But he wasn't going to get mixed up in that story. He had enough to worry about, bound to the Mór against his will as he was.

He led the girl to the tent, lifting the flap to show her the inside.

Before going in, she turned to face him. To Rook she

looked more intent, as if she'd finally shaken off the glamorie. "*Did* you know them? And what kind of hunt was that?" she demanded. "Why did the Lady kill the deer?"

Three questions in a row, from a girl just come through the Way, from *this* girl. The rule said he had to answer one of them. But they weren't well asked, so he could evade a true answer. "I do know something about your father, yes," he said, answering the first of her questions. Quickly, before she could demand more, he dropped the tent flap and stepped away. "Somebody will bring you something to eat later," he said over his shoulder. "You'd better sleep now."

There. He'd done as he'd been ordered, and goodbye to the girl Gwynnefar. Trouble, that's what she was, her and her spell-laden patched jacket and her dangerous questions. He'd stay out of the girl's way, as much as he possibly could. And avoid the Mór, too, before she gave him more impossible orders.

Maybe the girl really had seen Leaf Woman. He could find Leaf Woman's place of exile and hide there in his dog form, at least for a little while, until this dangerous girl had gone. The Mór hadn't given him any specific orders, now that he'd delivered the girl to her tent. He could push the boundaries of his oath that far, since she'd been careless.

Rook slipped around the corner of the girl's tent, heading for the edge of the forest not ten steps away.

As he went he eyed the black crow, one of the Mór's spies, that perched atop a tent pole, watching him. Then a heavy hand came down on his shoulder. Without looking to see who it was, Rook jerked away, but two hands gripped him and spun him around.

The wolf-guards.

"Where are you going, little Pucky?" the she-wolf asked. She squeezed his arm, right where she'd bitten him before.

"None of your business," Rook said, twisting his shoulders to try and break their grip.

"Quit your wiggling," the he-wolf said. "Should we bite him?" he asked his partner.

"Maybe later," she answered, grinning down at Rook. "The Mór Lady wants to see you, Puck."

Gripping his arms, the wolf-guards brought Rook to the Mór's tent. Another wolf-guard stood out in front of it. The she-wolf gave Rook a shove, right into the waiting guard's arms. He caught Rook, spun him around, and shoved him back at the other guards. Stumbling, Rook tried to duck away, putting his hand into his pocket. His shifter-bone was there, and the tooth. If he could shift, he could get away from these idiot wolves.

"The Lady wants him," the she-wolf said. She took hold of Rook's arm so he couldn't get his hand out of his pocket.

"Righty-o!" the other guard said. He grabbed Rook

by the hair and dragged him into the tent. When he let go and gave him a push, Rook stumbled onto his knees.

The Mór sat in the middle of the tent on a camp chair made of carved oak. A green carpet spangled with flowers lay on the floor; the silken walls of the tent gleamed pearly white with the morning light shining through them. On a wooden chest perched one of her watchers, a black crow running its beak through its feathers, preening. At the Mór's feet, a trembling maid pulled off her deerskin boots. Another maid stood at her elbow, holding a tray with a steaming cup on it. The maids were twins, twig-thin girls with wide black eyes and a single crow feather entwined in their tangled reddish-brown hair.

With a wave, the Mór dismissed the wolf-guards, who faded back to stand by the tent flap.

Rook got stiffly to his feet.

The Mór took the cup from the tray and the maid bowed her head and slipped away. As always, Rook, like all pucks, didn't have any trouble quickly seeing through the Mór's glamorie. To anyone else she looked noble and beautiful, brimming with power. A true Lady. To him, her skin looked pale and fragile, like old, crumpled paper. Her fingers were curled into claws around the teacup. The glamorie she'd stolen from the true Lady didn't fit her very well; it couldn't cover up what she truly was.

She regarded Rook through the steam rising from her cup. "You've been in trouble lately, haven't you? Pushing against the oaths that bind you?" As she held out the cup, the maid reappeared with the tray and took it. The other maid sat at the Mór's feet, gazing up at her with wide eyes. She saw only the glamorie, Rook knew.

The Mór leaned forward in her chair, her face suddenly icy cold. "You are valuable to me, Robin. Of all my people, you are the only one I trust to carry out my orders with intelligence, the only one who will not succumb to the wildling. Still, you will not argue with me again about the hunt. Understand?"

Rook controlled a shiver. "I do," he muttered. A direct order, so he had no choice but to obey. It bound him tighter than ropes. He shoved his hand into his pocket, felt the shifter-bone under his fingers.

The Mór pushed herself to her feet. The ice in her voice had melted. "Oh, Robin. You're not thinking of running away again, are you?"

He was *always* thinking of running away. She knew that well enough.

She nodded at the wolf-guards, who had been waiting by the tent flap.

Rook's fingers closed around the shifter-bone. As he pulled his hand out of his pocket, the three guards were on him. They grabbed him and flung him onto the ground. While he struggled, one held his arms, another his kicking legs, and the third dug into his pocket, pulling out the shifter-tooth.

"You can't take that," Rook gasped.

Without speaking, the wolf-guard grimly pried open Rook's fingers and took the bit of bone from his hand. The other two guards kept hold of Rook's arms and legs, while the third guard got to his feet and gave the shifter-bone and tooth to the Mór.

She nodded, and the wolf-guards let Rook go and stepped back. He scrambled to his feet, wincing because in the struggle the bites on his arms and chest had torn open again.

The Mór raised her eyebrows and lowered herself into her chair. "Well, Robin?"

He clenched his fists. With the tooth under his tongue he shifted into a dog; with the bone he became a tall black horse with a tangled mane and tail and sharp hooves. The shiftings were who he was—a puck. Without them he was . . .

He didn't know what he was. It was against every rule of the land for her to take them from him.

But he was bound by his oaths to her. He trembled, furious.

"I am doing this for your own good," the Mór said. "You are mine. Your struggles against your thrice-sworn oaths will only lead you to harm." The fox-maid appeared at her shoulder with a little box made of pale wood. The Mór put the shifters into the box and closed it, and the maid took it away. "Now," the Mór said, "about Gwynnefar. What has she said to you?"

"Oh, lots of things, *Lady*," Rook spat out. "She asks a lot of questions."

"Hmm." The Mór reached down and stroked the tangled hair of the other fox-girl crouched at her feet. The girl trembled under her touch. "What sorts of questions?"

"She asked about her father and mother. And about the hunt."

"Dangerous questions," she mused. After a moment, she went on. "You have a puck's keen vision, Robin. Can you see what she is?"

Rook waited a sullen moment before answering. "She is the daughter of a human man, of course," he muttered. He remembered how she'd hit the wolves with the branch. "She's a warrior, and her grandmother is a healer. She is the true Lady's daughter."

The Mór's eyes narrowed. "Not the *true* Lady. *I* am the true Lady of this land. Laurelin was weak, too young and foolish to rule. She wouldn't even wear the glamorie, as was her right. She was a healer, not a huntress."

Rook said nothing.

"Still," the Mór said, leaning back in her chair. "It is

as you say. Gwynnefar is Laurelin's daughter. As such she could be very useful to me. At the very least I can use her to open the Ways that are closed to me. But I have not yet decided how else she will serve me. Until I do, you will answer none of her questions and you will watch her for me."

"Find somebody else to do it," Rook snarled. "I don't want to."

The Mór raised her eyebrows. "I don't think you have any choice about it, Robin."

He felt the bindings of his thrice-sworn oath to her tighten around him. "What do you want with her, anyway? She doesn't know what she is. She's of no use to you."

"Even though you are young, you see more than you should, Robin. Your puck-brother was the same way." The Mór hunched her thin shoulders. "As I am sure you have noticed, my power grows weak. My people are wildling. My glamorie is failing. The lands slip into winter. Gwynnefar opened the Way. She does have power, Robin, and I want it. She could be a strong and loyal ally. But if she fails me . . ." The Mór's face hardened. "I took power from her mother. I can take it from the daughter as well."

❄ ❄ ❄

Fer woke up underwater. She blinked and rubbed her eyes. She took a breath. No, not underwater. It was the shimmering silk of her tent, turning the light greeny blue and watery.

She lay on the camp bed under clean silk sheets and a moss-green coverlet. Across the tent was a carved wooden chest; her backpack rested on its lid. On the floor was a carpet of a darker blue than the tent walls, with sleek blue and green fish swimming across it. From outside the tent came the sound of birdsong and distant voices talking. The air smelled of sun-warmed grass and wood smoke.

She gave a sigh, put her hands behind her head, and gazed up at the sloping tent ceiling. Things weren't as wonderful here as she thought they'd be. She couldn't forget about the bloody death of the stag in the clearing. He hadn't really been an animal, had he? Her stomach twisted just thinking about it. The Lady was beautiful and noble, though, so she must have a reason for the hunt, something Fer hadn't understood. Still, it made her feel sick and shivery. It was almost like she could still feel the stag's blood, seeping into the earth, tainting the land.

The hunt was wrong, but other parts of this place felt *right*, down to her bones in a way that home never had. The fern opening under her fingers in the spring-time forest felt right. Rook was right, even if he was snarly. Her father's note had said Fer belonged here. And maybe that was right too.

Thinking of her father made her think next of her mother, who had been the Lady's closest ally. Fer still didn't know enough about her parents, or what had happened to them. It was time to find out. Fer sat up and flung off the bedclothes.

A rippling at the tent flap, and a thin girl about Fer's age ducked inside. She was dressed in a simple white shift, had bare feet, and wore a black feather tangled in her red-brown hair.

"Hi," Fer said. Somebody who could answer her questions. The girl didn't say hi back. "Hel-*lo*," Fer said again.

The girl ducked her head and kept her eyes lowered. Didn't she talk? Crossing to the wooden chest, the girl dumped Fer's backpack on the floor and opened the chest's lid. From inside the chest she took slim black pants and a black shirt like the ones the Mór wore, and soft leather boots, and carried them to Fer.

Fer swung her legs over the side of the camp bed. "I brought my own stuff," she said. Pulling her nightgown down to cover her legs, she stood and fetched her backpack. She opened it and showed the maid-girl. "See?" She pulled out her jeans and a clean T-shirt and her patch-jacket. "And I have shoes." She pointed under the bed, where she'd left her sneakers, the socks balled up inside them. "Do you not talk at all?" she asked.

The girl's eyes grew wider, and she gave a trembling shake of her head.

Fer shrugged. She couldn't ask the girl any of her questions, then. "Turn around while I get changed." While the girl stood with her back turned, Fer pulled the nightgown over her head and got dressed. Sitting on the bed, she dug through the backpack. She'd forgotten to bring a hairbrush.

The girl reached into the pocket of her shift and brought out a comb. Her quick fingers pulled at Fer's hair.

"I can do that," Fer said, reaching for the comb.

The girl kept firm hold of it, pushing Fer's hand away, picking out the twigs that had gotten tangled in Fer's hair, carefully combing out the snarls.

"My name is Fer," Fer said. "I wish you could tell me your name."

The girl's hands stilled. Then she untangled something from Fer's hair and held it out to her. Fer took it. A twig. The girl reached out and tapped the twig, then nodded.

"Oh!" Fer smiled. "Your name is Twig?"

The girl nodded again, but didn't smile back. She finished with Fer's hair and stepped away.

Fer turned to face her and felt a faint connection spin out between herself and the other girl. Just like the stag in the clearing, but not so strong, just the merest cobweb of a thread. Fer closed her eyes and felt the other girl's half-wild heart fluttering with fright in her chest.

Fer opened her eyes. "It's all right, Twig," she whispered. "You don't have to be afraid of me."

Twig's eyes widened, she flinched away, and in a flash she was gone from the tent, breaking the thread.

Fer frowned. That was strange.

She ran her hands over her head. Her hair felt smooth, for once, pulled back into one neat braid. And tied at the bottom end of the braid—Fer pulled it around in front of her to see—was the black feather the Lady had given her the night before. The maid-girl's quick fingers must have taken it from Fer's backpack.

Fer looked up. Ducking under the tent flap, holding a tray, was Rook.

He would talk to her, anyway. Not like the strange maid-girl. "Hi," she said, giving him a smile.

He looked blankly back at her and set the tray down on the bed. "Here's food," he said.

Mmmm. Fer looked the tray over. A cup and a pot of something hot. A loaf of bread, a little wooden bowl of honey, and an apple. Crossing her legs, she pulled the tray closer and broke open the bread, then spread honey on it. She took a big bite. "Want some?" she asked Rook, who stood by the tent flap with his arms folded.

He shook his head, but didn't speak.

From outside the tent came the sound of banging and comings and goings. In the distance, a horse whinnied. "What's going on out there?" Fer asked.

Rook gave half a shrug. "Did you perhaps notice that we're living in a bunch of tents here?"

Fer took another bite of bread and honey. "Why are we living in a bunch of tents, Rook?" she asked. "Why doesn't the Lady live in a castle?"

"The Lady is on a progress," he answered.

"What's a progress?" Fer asked. She poured out tea, chamomile from the smell of it. She added honey to that, too.

"She's traveling, along with her retinue," Rook said. "Her guards and servants and all her people, the whole lot of us. The Lady has brought the spring to her own land, so we're getting ready to move to the next place so she can do the same thing there."

Next place? Fer froze with a bite of bread and honey halfway to her mouth. She'd be able to return to this place, wouldn't she? Return to the Way and go back to Grand-Jane, as she'd promised? "Where is the next place?" Fer asked.

Rook shrugged stiffly. "It is wherever it is," he said, his voice rough. "We'll know when we get there."

"Can I get home from there?" Fer asked.

"Full of questions, aren't you?" Rook sneered.

Fer examined Rook, and he gave her a narrow-eyed stare in return. He looked different than he had before. More sullenly surly, if such a thing was possible. "What's the matter, Rook?" she asked. Had something happened?

He didn't answer, just ducked out the tent flap. Fer heard his voice, and another voice answering. After a moment, he poked his head back inside. "Shift yourself," he said. "They're to take down the tent now."

Gulping down the last of her tea and shoving the apple into her backpack, Fer got to her feet. She buttoned up her jacket and followed Rook outside.

The sun, round and orange, was setting, throwing long, black shadows across the field. How could it be evening, when she'd just woken up and eaten breakfast? Time must pass differently here than it did at home.

She took a step forward and the tent behind her collapsed. Glancing over her shoulder, she saw two short men with spiky black hair and white muttonchop whiskers coiling ropes and collecting tent pegs. The men had pointy noses and flattish faces; they reminded Fer of badgers. One of them nodded to her, and the other gave her a half bow. Fer nodded back. Two other badger-men were folding up her camp bed and carrying the wooden chest to a waiting wagon. Rook took her backpack and handed it to one of the men, who added it to the wagon.

A white horse galloped past, riderless, trailing a silver-chain bridle from its mouth. Across the wide meadow, all the silken tents had been taken down. Fer saw Twig, with another brown-haired maid-girl just like her, climbing onto the back of a goat with huge, curling horns and a pair of saddlebags over its back. In the orange light of the setting sun, the goat's hair looked like flickering flames.

She followed Rook across the field. At the edge of the forest, where the evening shadows grew thick and dark, the Lady's retinue was gathered, milling around. All her *people*, Rook had said. The *others*, Grand-Jane had called them. Some of them, the ones on horseback, were tall and slender, almost like people, but too beautiful and too frail, with nut-brown skin and paper-white skin and skin tinged with the green of forest ferns. They wore masks made of bark and leaves and what looked to Fer like the fluttering wings of butterflies. Others were short and thin as saplings and rode goats and wore masks with six goat horns and a toothy goat mouth; others with whiskers and fur masks over their faces rode deer, clinging to the antlers; still others looked like naughty, sharp-faced boys and girls and crowded onto the backs of sturdy, shaggy ponies.

Other animals slunk around the riders and their mounts. A deer, a pair of greyhounds, a bristle-backed boar, a few cats, and—Fer caught her breath when she saw it—like a low shadow flowing along the ground, a sleek panther. Two wagons pulled by lop-eared goats stood in the middle of the throng. In the deepest shadows, Fer spotted a brown bear standing on its hind legs, as if watching over them all.

At the front of the retinue was the Lady, dressed all in black with a glowing crown on her head. A crow perched on her shoulder. She rode a different horse, this one as white as moonlight, with a long, braided mane and a tail that brushed the ground. Three gray wolves chased each other around her horse, wrestling, mock biting, tumbling each other under its legs. The horse stood steady, like a marble statue.

The last flames of sunset burned out in the sky.

eight

Fer followed Rook to the edge of the restless crowd, where a tall black horse, maybe the same one the Lady had been riding during the hunt the night before, was waiting. It wore no bridle and had no saddle. Its eyes, Fer noticed, were yellow, just like Rook's. Did horses usually have yellow eyes?

Rook went to the horse's head and lowered his own head, speaking quietly to it. Then, giving Fer a look of strong dislike, he pointed at the horse's back.

"Get up there," he ordered.

She looked him over. "Rook, *what* is the matter with you?" she asked him for the second time.

He frowned. "When the first star appears, we leave. If you're late, you'll be left behind."

The horse stamped a hoof and tossed its long, tangled mane, almost like it was telling her to hurry up. The horse's back looked awfully high off the ground. "How do I get up there?" she asked.

Rook blew out a sigh and left the horse's head. Bending, he made a step out of his laced fingers. "Put your foot here," he said, "grab the mane, and throw your other leg over."

Fer stepped into his hands and jumped up as he lifted, throwing her leg over as he'd said. The horse's back was sleek-black and slippery; she started to slide off the other side. She grabbed the mane with both hands and clung to it.

The horse snorted and shifted under her. She squeezed her legs. Its back was so wide; it was like perching on a slippery wine barrel. She glanced down, and the grassy ground seemed very far away. She squinted. It *was* far away.

At the soft *clop-clop* sound of hooves on grass, Fer looked up. The Lady, sitting straight and tall on the marble-white horse.

"Good evening to you, Gwynnefar," the Lady said with a smile.

Fer gulped. The Lady was so, so beautiful and queenly. Her crown, Fer realized, was made of oak twigs woven together, with green leaves budding from it. "Hi," Fer said. "Good evening, I mean." She felt herself staring and tried to look away, but couldn't.

The Lady's smile sharpened. "I hear my dearest friend's daughter has questions to which I may have answers."

She'd heard about Fer's questions? Had Rook told her? Fer shot him a quick glance, but he stood with his head lowered, his hand resting on the horse's neck.

"We will have more time to talk once we've arrived," the Lady said. She opened her mouth to say something else, then cocked her head, as if scenting a change in the breeze. "Ah. It is time. It's going to be quite a ride, Gwynnefar." She glanced at Rook. "Don't let her fall off, Robin."

"I won't," Rook said sullenly.

The Lady smiled across at Fer as if they were sharing a secret joke. "He's not the best mannered of my people, but he *will* do as he's told. Won't you, Robin?"

Rook nodded.

The Lady gave Fer another smile, then leaned forward and spoke into her horse's ear, and it turned and trotted toward the front of the retinue. Fer watched her go, then rubbed her eyes, blinking.

Rook left the horse's head and stood looking up at its back. After taking a deep breath, he grabbed the mane and the back of Fer's jacket and pulled himself on, scrambling until he was sitting behind Fer.

He didn't know any more than she did about how to get up onto a horse, did he? *Robin*, the Lady had called him. "Is Robin another one of your names, Rook?"

Without answering, Rook wrapped an arm around her waist, holding the mane with his other hand.

Around them, the retinue stilled. Shadows dropped from the eaves of the forest trees. Overhead the sky was deep blue-green where the sun had set, with black night creeping up from the opposite horizon.

A star blossomed in the east.

A horn sounded, a single winging note, and the gathered riders spurred their mounts.

At first they rode slowly, following the path through the darkening woods. They gathered speed, and the jolting rhythm turned to a gallop, the leaves and ferns and trees rushing and then flashing by in a blur of green and brown. The horse raced in a headlong, plunging run, its mane whipping across Fer's face like ribbons. Its hoofbeats on the path went *ba da la DUM, ba da la DUM.* Fer clung to the mane and caught quick, lurching glimpses between the horse's ears of the path ahead. Other riders dashed past, crouched low over the necks of their mounts, casting Fer curious looks over their shoulders and nodding to Rook, behind her.

The horse strained, galloping even faster. Fer felt its muscles bunching and smoothing beneath her legs. She closed her eyes. Rook wasn't supposed to let her fall off, but he didn't seem to be doing much to keep her on. *Hold on and don't fall off*, Fer told herself. *Hold on and don't fall off.* She clung to the mane with all her strength.

A jolt, and the horse's gait smoothed. Fer's eyes flew open. The forest flashed past again and disappeared, and they were bounding through the night sky. Her stomach lurched. Stars whirled past; bits and rags of clouds swirled around them and disappeared. Looking down, Fer saw stars below them too, and velvety black darkness. The other mounts and riders rushed around them, shadows in the night. The horn sounded again, a thin ringing in the distance. Far ahead gleamed a white light, brighter than the stars. The Lady's crown, blazing the way, leading them.

Fer caught her breath. The horse's run was like rocking now, and she was balanced, relaxed, really riding, not just holding on. For a moment she saw herself as she must look—a wild girl on the back of a wild horse galloping through the air. Excitement bubbled up inside her—*faster, faster!*

The horse's muscles bunched and strained again, and they raced into a blinding fog that streamed around them. The wind howled past, snatching the breath from Fer's mouth. The wind grew colder until the horse was snorting out great clouds of steam. Its mane slashed Fer across the face; her eyes watered from the wind. The wind was strong enough to cut right through her, but the patch-jacket kept her warm. The fog flashed past and they were in icy darkness again.

She felt a bump on her shoulder—Rook's head bumping her—and then his hand slipped from the mane.

Fer half turned to see him sliding sideways off the horse's back, his head lowered. "Rook!" she shouted. His head came up and he flung out a hand, but he slipped further. Dark, empty space yawned below, waiting to swallow him up. Holding the mane with one hand, Fer reached down and grabbed him by the front of his shirt, dragging him back onto the horse. She brought his limp arm around and closed his cold fingers on the mane. "Hold on!" she shouted, her words whipped away by the wind. His head bumped against her back again and his fingers loosened.

She glanced over her shoulder. His eyes were closed, his face set and pale. The jolting must have hurt his wolf bites. He couldn't hold on anymore.

"Hold on to me!" she shouted, and spit strands of the mane out of her mouth. She reached back and brought each of his arms around so he was holding on to her waist. She, in turn, would keep them on the horse.

"Just hold on," she told herself. She bent lower over the horse's neck, trying to find the balance again. Rook's arms stayed wrapped around her waist, his head resting against her shoulder.

Fer's arms and shoulders felt the strain from gripping

the mane so tightly. On and on the horse ran through the empty night. Cramps set into her fingers. Her eyes ran with tears, but she didn't dare loose her grip on the mane to wipe them. The muscles in her legs burned.

At last the horse slowed. The darkness turned pearly white, as if they were running inside a cloud. Around them the other riders were dark shadows that ran swiftly, but silently. Then they faded away into the whiteness. The horse slowed even more, and the wind died, and then, with a jolt, the horse's hooves hit the ground and they were trot-walking through an empty white field. Snow, Fer realized. The horse stumbled to a stop and stood with its head down, blowing hard.

Rook's arms loosened and he slid off, leaning against the horse, clinging to its mane to keep himself on his feet. Fer dismounted on the other side. Her quivering legs held her for a moment, and then she fell onto the snowy ground.

Catching her breath, she got shakily to her feet, dusted snow off her jeans, and regarded Rook across the horse's back. He stood with his head lowered, his fingers entwined in the mane. "Are you all right?" she asked. A gust of steam came out with her words; the air was icy cold.

He didn't answer.

Fer reached out to touch a wet patch on his shirt-sleeve. Her fingers came away red with blood.

He jerked away. "Leave it," he growled. He raised

his head. His face was chalky white, but his yellow eyes were fierce.

She held up her hand to show him the blood. "Rook, Grand-Jane made me learn a bunch of different healing spells," she said. She didn't have Grand-Jane's power or knowledge, but her spells might help a little, especially if she could find her backpack and use the magical herbs she had in there. "I can help."

"You've helped enough already," Rook muttered. "Just leave me alone."

"If I'd left you alone up there," Fer pointed, "you would have fallen off the horse." She looked up. The sky was flushed with pink. Sunrise. So they'd ridden all night. "What if you *had* fallen off during the ride, Rook?"

He rested his forehead against the horse's sweating flank and didn't answer.

"Well?" Fer asked. "What?"

"I would've turned to dust," he mumbled without looking up.

Fer nodded. So she'd saved his life. A second time.

nine

Fer opened her mouth to ask Rook, for the third time, what was the matter with him—besides the wolf bites, because it wasn't just that—when the horse snorted and raised its head. Fer looked to see what had disturbed it.

Across the field, emerging from a snow-covered pine forest, was the Lady's retinue. They trotted, plumes of steam coming from the noses of the mounts, their hooves kicking up clots of snow. The retinue halted, milling around. The bear shambled off among the trees, followed by the panther and a few of the deer. Some of the Lady's people jumped off the horses and deer and goats they'd been riding; others, on horseback, clustered around the Lady as if receiving orders, and then rode into the forest. The wagons pulled up and things were flung out, and almost immediately a tent started to go up.

Fer bent and wiped Rook's blood off her hand, onto the snow. "Are you coming?" she asked.

Rook nodded. "The Lady will want to see you."

"I want to see her, too," Fer said. It was time to get some answers about her mother and father, and about who she really was. The Lady had answers.

After slogging across the field, Fer found her blue tent, just inside the forest next to a few paper-white birch trees bent low under their load of snow. Rook trudged off to look after the horse—and himself, too, she hoped—and she ducked inside. The snow had been cleared off the patch of ground where the tent had been set up, and the blue-green fish carpet laid down. Other carpets had been hung against the walls, to keep the cold air out, Fer guessed. A fire burned in a brazier in the corner, next to the trunk. The camp bed had a few more coverlets layered on it and, Fer was glad to see, her backpack.

She sat down with a sigh on the bed and peeled the wet sneakers and socks off her feet, which were red with cold. With the carpets on the walls shutting out the morning light, the tent felt like a cave. She lay back on the bed. They'd ridden all night. *All night.* She shook her head wonderingly. She'd ridden a horse that had flown through the sky and brought her from the freshness of spring into the depths of winter. She closed her eyes, feeling again the rush of icy wind around her, seeing the brilliant stars shoot past.

When she woke up, the fire in the brazier had burned down to a couple of red coals, and the tent was dark. She shivered. She'd slept the entire day away. She sat up and stretched, her shoulders stiff from clinging to the horse's mane during the wild ride.

Her stomach growled.

If somebody wasn't going to bring her something to eat, she'd have to go find it. She bent over and rummaged in her backpack for the other pair of socks that Grand-Jane had packed. There they were, knitted from warm, red wool. Fer started to pull one on when she caught a whiff of a dusty-sweet smell, and something poked her foot. Reaching into the sock, she pulled out a sprig of dried lavender.

Even in the dim tent, Fer could see the purple flowers clustered like tiny bells at the end of the stalk. Grand-Jane had harvested this herself on a summer morning after three days of clear weather, gathering the bees about her, waiting for the dew to dry before cutting the lavender. She'd hung it up in a bundle in the stillroom until it had dried. And then she'd put this sprig into Fer's sock drawer. Lavender for protection and peace.

Suddenly Fer felt very, very far away from Grand-Jane and their little house at the end of the rutted driveway.

How much time had passed in her own world since she'd jumped into the pool? She took a shaky breath. Had spring come yet back home? Had Grand-Jane dug up the herb garden? Were the bees waking up in their hives? She closed her eyes, imagining Grand-Jane in her warm, red-and-yellow kitchen, drinking a cup of herb tea at the table, stirring in a spoonful of honey.

From outside came the crunch of footsteps on snow; as Fer opened her eyes, the tent flap lifted and a dark shadow ducked inside, bringing with it a gust of icy-cold air.

Fer tucked the sprig of lavender into her patch-jacket pocket, next to the protective spell-bag. "Is that you, Rook?" she asked, and started pulling on her socks and sneakers.

"It is," his rough voice answered. "The Lady invites you to join her for the evening meal."

So formal. Fer got to her feet and straightened her patch-jacket. She examined Rook, squinting to see him better in the dim light. He looked as formal as he sounded, wearing his black uniform coat with the Lady's black feather pinned to the sleeve. He looked better than he had before, not as pale.

Fer stepped out of the tent and caught her breath. The Lady's encampment had been set up just inside the forest among the pine trees. Lanterns hung from the tree branches, and the snow glimmered pink in their light.

Paths had been tramped down in the deep snow, leading from one brightly colored tent to the next. It was lovely.

Still, something about it felt not quite right. Fer paused and cocked her head, as if she might be able to *hear* something wrong. The winter felt like it was . . . waiting for something. The hard nubbles of tree buds should be swelling with springtime. Icicles should be dripping in a warming breeze. But all was still and icy cold. Winter had overstayed its time in this land.

Fer shook her head, trying to shake away the feeling of wrongness. Her breath steaming in the cold, her hands shoved into her jacket pockets, Fer followed Rook along the paths to the Lady's tent.

Two wolf-guards waited out front. They nudged each other as Fer and Rook approached, but let them pass inside without comment. In the tent, the Lady waited at a folding table set for two with plates carved out of dark wood. On the back of one of the chairs perched a crow, its black feathers gleaming in the candlelight.

As Fer and Rook entered, the Lady rose to her feet. Fer stared at her. She could almost see the Lady glowing with beauty. Just like her father's letter had described when he saw her mother. Did the Lady have the thing her father had mentioned—a glamorie? The Lady embraced her and bent to kiss her on her forehead, as she'd done in the moonlit clearing at the end of the stag hunt. Fer shivered and she felt something drop over her like a net made of ice crystals. Was it the glamorie? The questions she'd been wanting to ask melted away.

"Gwynnefar," the Lady said. She examined Fer with eyes that seemed like the midnight sky, full of stars. "That is a motley coat you wear. I will send you something better. And I see you've lost your black feather."

Fer ran her hands over her head. During the ride, her braid had loosened, and bits of flyaway hair stuck out. The black feather was missing from the end of the braid.

The Lady nodded at Rook, who stood near the door. "Dinner now, Robin." Rook bowed and went out of the tent. "Come and sit down, Gwynnefar," she said, pointing to the table. She sat down, and the crow fluttered up to perch on her shoulder.

Trying not to stare too hard at the Lady's pale, flawless face, Fer sat. The tent was snug and warm, with carpets on the walls just like her own tent, but the colors were green and gold, the colors of spring. "Is Rook going to eat dinner with us?" she asked.

The Lady raised her eyebrows. "I heard you like to ask questions."

Fer nodded. "That's because I have a lot of them." Mostly she wanted to know what had happened to her father and her mother. And about the stag hunt.

"Well," the Lady said, "I will answer one question

now. I expect you want to know who I am and what my purpose is."

That hadn't been what Fer was going to ask. Still, she did want to know the answer. She nodded.

"Then I shall answer," the Lady said, as if giving Fer a present. "Each part of this land and its people is ruled by a different Lord or Lady. The Lord or Lady's people swear him or her an oath of service, and in turn, she rules them. I am the Lady of the place where the Way that you opened is located. I travel from one land to another to bring the spring to those places because I alone, of all the Lords and Ladies, have that power."

Fer opened her mouth to ask *Why do you have that power, and nobody else?* but before she could get out the question, Rook came back into the tent followed by Twig, or the other girl who looked like Twig, who carried a tray full of food. While the girl held the tray, Rook unloaded the food onto the table; the girl left and Rook went to stand by the tent flap.

The Lady placed a whole cooked fish on Fer's plate, then added bread and butter and a little pile of stewed apples. On her shoulder, the crow cocked its head and fixed Fer with a bright-eyed stare.

Just like Grand-Jane, Fer was a vegetarian. She pushed the silver-scaled fish aside with her fork and took a bite of the apples. They'd been cooked in honey. Sweet. Fer took another bite, still gazing at the Lady.

"Eat your fish," the Lady ordered.

As ordered, Fer took a bite of fish. It tasted salty and gluey on her tongue. No. Wait. She wrenched her gaze away from the Lady and looked down at the fish on her plate; its death-frosted eye stared back at her. She couldn't believe she had taken a bite. She struggled to remember what she'd come here for. Clearly the Lady didn't want her to ask questions, but she would do it anyway.

Keeping her eye on the dead fish's eye, Fer said slowly, "I have another question. What happened to my mother and father?"

The Lady didn't answer.

Taking a deep breath, Fer asked a second time. "What happened to my parents?"

More silence from the Lady.

If she asked a third time, the Lady had to answer—that was the rule, Grand-Jane had said. She risked a glance at the Lady, and she caught a quick glimpse as a shadow crossed her face. For a second the Lady looked different, as if her pale face was a mask cut out of paper, with some wild, black creature peering out of the dark eyeholes. Fer opened her mouth to ask her question the third time.

"Do not dare to compel an answer from me," the Lady said, her voice a harsh croak.

Fer shivered. The feeling of wrongness twisted in her stomach again.

Then the Lady waved her hand, as if she was adjusting the mask, and she shone with beauty again. The glamorie—it had to be. She cleared her throat. "But I will tell you about your father and mother, Gwynnefar," she said at last. "It is a sad story. I, ah, do not like to talk about it. Are you certain you wish to hear it?"

"Of course I do," Fer said firmly. "It's one of the reasons I came here."

"If you insist." The Lady nodded gracefully. "It happened long ago, just after you were born. As you know, your father, Owen, was a human. Your mother was my most trusted ally, my huntress. One night she went out hunting with bow and arrow, and—I do not know how it happened, but she shot Owen by mistake, killing him. In remorse, she cast herself into a freezing lake and died."

Fer stared at the Lady. That wasn't the whole story. It couldn't be. Her father's letter had made it clear that he and her mother had been fighting against something. Laurelin couldn't have killed him after that, even by accident.

She closed her eyes and saw the lovely young woman step out of the moon-pool, and this time she imagined Owen with her, just like in the photograph, tall and a little awkward looking. Neither of them much older than she was now. In her heart she felt a sharp pain, missing them, even though she'd never known them. "I wish I'd met them," she whispered.

"I am sure you do," the Lady said. Then she went on quickly. "The question now is, what are we to do with you now that you are here?"

Fer blinked. Since she had come to this place, she'd felt the land calling to her, trying to tell her something. "I think—" Fer began, then hesitated.

The Lady cocked her head, listening, just like one of her black crows.

"There's something I'm supposed to do here," Fer said slowly.

"Of course there is something you must do, Gwynnefar," the Lady said. "You are to serve me, as your mother did."

The Lady smiled, the glamorie glistened again, and Fer's doubts melted away. "Serve you, yes, Lady," Fer agreed, looking into the Lady's eyes. Yes, she would serve the Lady, just as her mother had done.

Across the table from her, the Lady's eyes sparkled. "Good. Your mother was a warrior, as I am, and so are you meant to be. I have much to teach you, and I am certain you will learn fast. We will start with riding." She shot Rook a glance, and then looked back at Fer. "I even have a present for you. A horse. The one that carried you during the ride."

By the tent flap, Rook stiffened. His mouth opened, as if he was about to protest, but then his face went blank and he closed it again.

The Lady glanced at him. "Something to say, Robin?"

He shook his head.

"Good," the Lady said. She got to her feet and went to a trunk, the twin of the one in Fer's tent. Opening the lid, she took out a small box made of pale wood and gave it a little shake. It made a rattling sound. With a half smile on her face, she set the box aside, then pulled out what looked to Fer like a stick about as long as her arm.

"The horse is named Phouka," the Lady said. She held the stick out to Fer, who took it. No, not a stick, a short whip, stiff and made of braided leather. "Phouka is not malicious," the Lady went on, "but he can be tricksy. A few touches with the whip will teach him manners." She turned and reached back into the trunk. "And this," she said, pulling out another black feather, like the one she'd given Fer before.

Fer took it.

"Try not to lose it, Gwynnefar," the Lady said.

There was silence for a moment. Fer stared up into the Lady's mirror-silver eyes. She blinked and saw the beautiful Lady's face and, behind it, a frightening, empty-eyed face. Her head spun.

The Lady put her hands on Fer's shoulders, steadying her. "I have just given you four presents, Gwynnefar. Surely you have been taught how to behave properly."

Fer felt a headache building behind her eyes. Four presents? The horse named Phouka, the feather, the whip and . . . ? Oh, the answer to a question, even though it wasn't one she had asked. "Thank you," Fer said.

"Very good." The Lady turned Fer and pushed her toward the tent flap. "I have some things to see to. Robin will make sure you get back to your tent safely."

A few steps and Fer found herself outside the Lady's tent, Rook beside her. She blinked, feeling as though she'd just woken up from a dream.

The camp's lanterns had been put out. Overhead the sky arched dark and full of stars, except for a wedge of moon. Days had passed, Fer realized, since the moon had been full and fat; it was waning toward crescent, and then it would turn toward dark again.

She rubbed her temples as the Lady's glamorie faded, along with her headache. Her stomach twisted with worry.

A Lady so beautiful, who had been her mother's friend, couldn't be lying, but something was wrong here. Really wrong. Fer wanted to be alone in her tent so she could go over the conversation with the Lady again. The Lady was bright and beautiful, but she'd been twisty, too. Thinking straight around her was hard. Fer had even eaten meat, even though she'd never done that before. Suddenly Fer missed Grand-Jane very much.

She put the Lady's feather in her patch-jacket pocket, next to the sprig of lavender and the spell-bag of protective herbs. Then she looked down at the whip. She fitted her hand over its grip. There was no way she was ever going to hit the horse with this. But the Lady had given it to her, and she'd notice if Fer didn't have it anymore, so she couldn't throw it away.

Beside her, Rook took a breath, as if he was about to say something.

Fer glanced aside at him. "What?" She dared to ask him a third time. "Rook, you have to tell me. What's the matter?"

He flinched, as if she'd slapped him. "I can't tell you anything," he said.

"Isn't that the rule?" she asked. "I asked three times, so you have to answer?"

"Stop asking, Fer," he snarled. In the dim light, his yellow eyes gleamed, as if they had flickers of flame burning in them. "I'm thrice-sworn to her," he said. "I'm under her orders to watch you and report to her and to tell you nothing. No matter what, I can't answer any of your questions."

ten

Thrice-sworn? What did that mean, exactly? From what Grand-Jane had told Fer about the rules of the land, and from what she'd seen here so far, any oath had power. An oath given three times? It had to bind the one who'd given it tighter than knotted ropes. Fer turned to face Rook. "All right," she said. "What about this, Rook. You are sworn to the Lady, but I saved your life, remember? Not just once, but two times."

He nodded.

"Okay," Fer went on. "You owe me for that. What if I said you had to pay me back by answering a question?"

He went a little more pale.

"You'd have to answer, wouldn't you?" she pushed.

He stared at her, looking angry and a little sick.

She assumed this meant the rules of this place might make his head explode. "Rook, I keep trying to ask questions," she said, "but instead of answers all I get is more questions. I want to know if my mother really did accidentally kill my father. I want to know why the Lady killed the stag in the clearing. That killing didn't feel right, Rook, it felt like she was killing a person, not an animal. I want to know who that Leaf Woman was that I met in the forest. I want to know why the Lady wanted me to come through the Way, if she's just going to set people spying on me. I want to know who I am and why I'm here."

"I can't—" Rook started.

"I *know*," Fer interrupted. "You can't answer. I wasn't asking, Rook. I'm just telling you. I know something's wrong here, I can feel it, and I'm going to find out what it is." She set off down the snowy path, and after a moment, Rook followed.

At her tent, somebody was waiting. One of the Lady's maid-girls wrapped in a woolen blanket. She stood shivering, holding a lantern that made a circle of light in the darkness.

"Hi, Twig," Fer said.

The maid-girl shivered; she glanced at Rook and then ducked her head. "I'm not Twig. She's my sister.

I'm Burr." She leaned in to whisper to Fer. "Tell him to go away." She flicked her fingers toward Rook.

Fer shot him a quick look. "Why?"

The maid-girl shivered. "You should be careful. The puck is hers."

"I know he is," Fer said. "What do you want?"

"I saw something," Burr said. "In your bag. You have herbs. Things in a box. You are a healer."

"I'm not—" Fer started to say. "Well, only a little. I'm not very good yet."

"Oh," Burr said, and her voice was the merest breath. "I need a healer. Twig is sick. I need a healer to help her."

Fer blinked. She wasn't really a healer, not like Grand-Jane, but she might be able to help. "All right," she said. "Just wait a second." Ducking into her tent, she went to her backpack and dug out the OWEN box. Grand-Jane had put herbs in it, and if Twig was sick she'd need them. She stepped back outside. "Take me to her," she told Burr.

They were just setting off through the snow when one of the Lady's black crows spiraled down and perched on a nearby branch. It cocked its head, watching them with a sharp eye.

"Wait," Rook ordered. He bent and packed snow into a ball, then stood and flung it at the crow. The snowball splatted into the crow's breast, and with a squawk and a swirl of feathers, it fell off its perch. "All right," Rook said, wiping his wet hands on his coat. "Let's go."

At first Fer and Rook and Burr followed the paths in the encampment, but then Burr led them past the tents onto a different path, not so well traveled. They walked under the dark pine branches, through a forest blanketed with silence and snow. The icy-cold air went into Fer's lungs and puffed out as clouds of steam. Against such cold her patchwork jacket shouldn't have been much protection, but even so, she felt comfortably warm. Maybe the spells Grand-Jane had stitched into the patches had more power here, on the other side of the Way.

The path led deeper into the forest. The legs of Fer's jeans were caked with snow up to the knees, and snow had gotten inside her sneakers. High up in the fir trees the wind blew, sending icy crystals sifting down.

Ahead of her, Burr stopped. "Here," she whispered, holding up the lantern. Its yellow light flickered over a huge pine tree covered with a thick layer of snow, its branches bent to the ground.

"Where?" Fer asked, and her voice sounded loud in the silence.

As an answer, Burr pulled one of the tree branches aside and ducked underneath, taking the light of the lantern with her. Fer followed. The tree's heavy branches, weighted to the ground by snow, made a snug tent held up by the rough-barked trunk. The ground underneath was covered with soft pine needles.

On a bed of pine branches lay Twig, covered with a brown woolen blanket. Burr crouched next to her and set the lantern by her head.

Rook ducked into the tree-tent. Fer handed him the OWEN box to hold, and crawled over to take a look at Twig.

Burr's thin hands brushed Twig's hair off her forehead; she watched Fer with wide, frightened eyes. "See? Can you help her?"

In the warm glow of the lantern, Twig looked flushed, her face pinch-thin, her mouth open, panting.

Grand-Jane had taught Fer how to check for fever. She leaned forward and touched her lips to Twig's forehead. Better than checking with her cold hands. Twig's skin felt hot and damp. Fer took the girl's face in her hands and stared into her glittering eyes. Something looked back, something wild. Fer tried her magic seeing trick, turning her head to peer at Twig out of the corners of her eyes. For just a moment she saw a sharp, foxy face with black eyes and, poking up through the tangled hair, pointed ears with a tuft of fur at their tips.

Fer blinked. "What is that?"

"She's wildling," Burr whispered.

Fer patted Twig's face and picked up her hand. "What's wildling?"

Burr gazed at her with wide eyes. "Wildling is bad.

Things are falling apart. Things should be held together."

Were things falling apart? Fer wanted to ask, gazing back at the other girl. Was this the wrongness she felt? She had a feeling Burr wouldn't be able to answer that question. "Rook, look in the box and find the bags of herbs," she said.

Rook shook his head. "You can't help her if she's wildling," he said, his voice rough.

"I can at least try," Fer said. Twig's hand was hot too, and when glimpsed sidelong looked more like a paw than a girl's hand. "Burr, can you find me a rock or something to grind the herbs on?"

Burr nodded and crawled out of the tree-tent.

Whatever wrongness caused wildling, it looked like a fever, and she knew what to do about that. One of the things you had to do, if the fever was very high, was to call the sick person back to herself. Grand-Jane had told her that the people of this land had animal or plant selves. Wildling looked like the person part of the person was being lost. Turning wild again. The person part had to be called back, to heal the wildling.

"Those wolf-guards are wildlings too, aren't they?" Fer guessed, not expecting Rook to answer.

He didn't.

Burr crawled back into the tree-tent and gave Fer a stone, round and gray, as if it'd been smoothed in a river, and cold from the icy night outside. Fer took the bags of herbs and roots and seeds that Rook handed her. The bags were made of cloth—Grand-Jane didn't like to store magical herbs in plastic—and each one had a label stitched on it. *Comfrey, willow bark, mugwort, cinquefoil, yarrow.* Some of the bags clinked. They had tinctured herbs in them, stored in glass vials.

"And the honey," she told Rook. She held out her hand.

Rook didn't answer or hand her the honey. He was crouched on the pine-needle floor with the box open before him. From it he'd taken the round gray stone with the hole in it; he held it in his hand, staring down at it.

"What?" Fer said.

Burr stared too. "Where did you get that?" she whispered.

Fer took the stone from Rook's hand. "This?" She held it up. "I think it was my father's. The stuff in the box was his."

"It's magic," Burr breathed.

Rook shook his head. "It's dangerous."

"What does it do?" Fer asked.

As an answer, Burr made a circle with her thumb and forefinger and held it up to her eye.

Back home, Fer had tried looking through the hole-stone, but she hadn't seen anything different. With a shrug, she held the stone up to her eye and looked through it. Nothing. Then her gaze fell on Twig. Even without the turning-head trick, she could clearly see the wildling girl, the sharp, foxy muzzle, the bead-black eyes, the hands curling into paws where they rested on the blanket.

She turned the magic look onto Burr. The other girl still looked like a girl, but with her features a little too sharp, and just the hint of brown-red fur along her hairline. "It shows things as they really are," Fer realized. "You're wildling too, Burr."

The girl's eyes grew wide and filled with tears.

Fer lowered the stone and turned to Rook. "Do you want me to look at you?"

"I do." He gave a curt nod. "Just get on with it."

She raised the seeing-stone again and examined him. Same shaggy black hair hanging down into narrowed yellow eyes. His eyebrows winged up—she hadn't noticed that before. Same stubborn set to his frowning mouth. And still too pale, as if his wolf bites were hurting more than they should be. She blinked and saw, behind his face, what he would look like as a horse and as a shaggy black dog. But they weren't wildling creatures, they were just him. She lowered the stone.

"Well?" he asked, his voice tense. "What did you see?"

"You're not wildling," she answered. "You're just you." She put the seeing-stone into her jacket pocket. "I do wonder how you change from a boy into a dog or a horse, though."

His sigh sounded like relief. "Keep wondering," he muttered.

Fer grinned, and he scowled back. "Can I have the honey now?" she asked.

He dug in the box, pushing aside the crow feather and the photograph of her father, and found the screw-top jar of honey that Grand-Jane had put in. Fer opened it and dipped her finger in. The taste reminded her of summer days when the heat shimmered above the clover field. The bees wove their own kind of magic as they zoomed around the fields, working hard all day long, then settling quietly into their hives when the sun set and the cooler night came on.

Grand-Jane's magic, her honey and herbs and stitchery spells, were all about safety and protection, all about home, and home magic was the opposite of wildling. It might be just what Twig needed.

The smooth stone would work for a mortar and the round seeing-stone for a pestle. Fer spilled a few drops of honey onto the mortar-stone and added a few pinches of mugwort and yarrow and, as a febrifuge, some of the dried willow bark. The herbs would be better macerated—that's what Grand-Jane would say— but she didn't have time for that, or the boiling water.

Twig would just have to take the herbs as medicine, and Fer would hope for the best.

When the herbs and honey were ground to a sticky paste, Fer turned to Rook and Burr. "She might not want to take it," she said, "so you'd better hold her still."

Burr and Rook crouched at Twig's sides and held her arms. Fer scooped up a fingerful of the herb paste and said a quick healing spell over it. As she brought the paste to Twig's mouth, the girl turned her face away, then struggled against the holding hands, snarling, rolling her eyes, snapping at Fer's hand.

Fer leaned over Twig and gripped her hair, staring down into her wild eyes. "It's medicine," she shouted, trying to see past the wild animal to the girl behind it. There she was, scared, hiding from her wildling self. "It's medicine, Twig," Fer said again, more softly.

Twig stilled and opened her mouth. Fer gave her the paste and Twig swallowed it. After a few moments her eyelids fluttered and closed, and she breathed out a deep sigh.

Fer sat back. Then she scraped up the rest of the paste from the mortar stone and put her other hand on Burr's shoulder. "Now you, to stop your wildling too."

Obediently Burr opened her mouth, and Fer gave her the herbs.

"It's sweet," Burr said, licking her lips.

"Grand-Jane's honey," Fer said. She put the bags of herbs and bottles of tincture back in the box.

"Did it work?" Burr asked.

"I don't know," Fer said. With the edge of her T-shirt she wiped the herb paste off the seeing-stone and held it up to her eye. Through it, she saw Twig sleeping peacefully. Already the girl's face was less foxy; the ears didn't poke up through the red-brown hair, and they weren't pointed and tipped with fur. Fer turned the seeing-stone on Burr, and her wildling had stopped too. Fer blinked and lowered the stone. "It worked already," she said. It really was magic. Strange. She put the stone into the OWEN box and stuffed the box into her backpack. She started to crawl toward the way out.

Burr's thin hand stopped her. "I owe you an oath for this," she said softly. "And Twig will give you hers."

Fer gulped. "Oh, no. No thanks, Burr." She didn't want anyone swearing oaths to her.

"But we owe it to you," Burr said, her eyes wide. "You know we do."

"No," Fer said again, more firmly. As she gazed at Burr and her sleeping sister, she felt her connection to them snap into place. Stronger than thread this time, and more certain. "You can choose, Burr," Fer said firmly. "I did you a favor, and you can decide if you want to do one for me sometime, but you don't have to. Okay?"

Her hands clenched, Burr stared at Fer.

"She doesn't understand," Rook said roughly. "Just let her swear an oath."

"This is *my* rule, Rook," Fer said. She nodded to herself. Yes, she was right about this. "Burr can choose for herself."

eleven

After seeing Fer safely to her tent, as he'd been ordered to do, Rook stopped on the snowy path on the way to the Mór's tent. From that direction came the sound of drumming; through the trees he saw the flickering light of a bonfire and wildly dancing shadows. The Huldre, the Lady of the land they'd just arrived at, and her people, had come to meet the Mór, then, to barter with her for the bringing of spring.

Rook didn't know for sure, but he suspected that the Mór had hunted the true Lady and her human lover, and had spilled their blood on the land. That would explain why the Leaf Woman, who made the seasons turn, had fled into exile. If the Lady's blood had been spilled in the Mór's hunt, it was an abomination, a stain that seeped through the land and stopped the wheel of the seasons from turning. Spring would not come to any of the lands as it had before.

So the Mór had discovered a new way to bring the spring. She had offered blood sacrifice. It was an old magic, blood for blood, and the Mór had been strong with power at first, but her power was ebbing away, the blood stained the land, and its people were wildling. The land and its people needed a true Lady to save them.

And Fer was the true Lady's daughter.

Rook glanced back at the girl's tent. He wasn't sure what to think about her. Before, he had thought her too weak and ignorant to help, and after the stag hunt she had seemed as blinded by the glamorie as any of the Mór's people. It was clear that she had no idea who she really was. But she had battled the wolves to save him. She'd stayed on Phouka during the wild ride, which was more than he had managed to do. Rook had thought the last thing he ever saw would be the fierce girl reaching down from Phouka's back, but then she'd gripped his shirt and pulled him out of the darkness.

And she was Fer, too. A skinny, honey-haired healer-girl who dared to ask questions even of the Mór, and whose herbs and spells and gray seeing-stone had greater power than she realized.

Gwynnefar frightened him. But he trusted Fer. He

didn't know why he trusted her, but he *did*.

He shook his head, which had started aching again. He was a puck, and he shouldn't trust anyone except for his puck-brothers, and they were far away and couldn't help him now. He headed down the path toward the Mór's tent. A crow flapped over his head, the spy he'd thrown a snowball at before. It jeered at him, then went to perch on a tent pole. In the clearing before the tent, the snow had been trampled down and a bonfire lit. The wood had come from dead pine trees, and it snapped and crackled and sent sparks whirling into the night sky. Three drummers crouched at the edge of the dancing, hammering with short sticks on their drums. The sound came up through the ground and through Rook's feet, pounding along with his headache.

Around the fire the Mór's people danced, all rags and shadows. Some of them were naked but painted with ash and blood and stripes of black from burnt sticks; others wore fur or ragged finery. They all wore masks made of fur or feathers or leaves.

What would Fer see if she looked at them through her seeing-stone? Most likely the same thing he saw with his puck vision. They were wildling, most of them, and they'd been getting worse lately. They served a usurper, a false Lady, so they were coming unbound from their oaths and rules. Some of them were probably burning with the same fever that Twig was.

The Huldre's people seemed wary. Maybe they could feel the wrongness about the Mór's people. They didn't join in the dancing and drumming, but stood at the edge of the clearing, watching: the little nisse in their red caps and long white beards, and the golden-haired grim who should have been fiddling along with the drums, and the nökk, who looked like big-eared old men with green eyes and gray beards dripping with icicles. In the shadows beyond the fire, deeper in the trees, the Huldre's trolls lurked. Some of them had three heads; some just one head on hulking, bent shoulders. Their skin was the mottled gray of stones, and they had bowed stumpy legs, and arms long enough that their knuckles dragged in the snow when they walked.

Rook slunk along the edge of the clearing to the Mór's tent. Two wolf-guards lounged in front of the door, watching the dancers. Rook tried to duck past them into the tent, but the she-wolf grabbed his arm.

"Hey-ho, Puck-puppy!" she said, grinning. "What're you up to?"

The bites on his arm burned under her gripping hand, and his head spun for a second. "Get off," he growled, and jerked out of her grasp.

And then—*slam*—he found himself flat on his back in the snow, with the other wolf-guard snarling down into his face. Slavering jaws snapped a finger's width from his nose.

"Hold on, hold on," the she-wolf guard grunted, and knotted her hand in her partner's shirt collar, pulling him off.

Rook scrambled away.

The he-wolf guard crouched in the snow. His black eyes glittered and he panted. His partner kept a tight grip on his collar, holding him back. He wasn't a person anymore, Rook realized, he was a wolf dressed up as a person.

Rook got to his feet, all of his wolf bites aching. "He's wildling," he said.

The she-wolf guard shrugged. "Nothing we can do about it, Puck, is there?"

"There is, yes," his mouth said, before his brain caught up.

"Yeah?" the she-wolf asked. She pulled on her partner's arm, forcing him to stand, which he did, shaking his shaggy head.

Rook nodded. He could tell her. The Mór hadn't ordered him not to. "Ask the Fer-girl for help," he said, and ducked into the tent.

As the hanging carpet blocking the worst of the cold from the tent swung back into place, the sound of drumming

and dancing from outside was muffled. The tent itself
was lit warmly by a few lanterns and two braziers full
of hot coals. In the middle of the tent sat the Mór on a
camp chair draped with a carpet so that it looked like
a throne. One of her crows crouched on the arm of the
chair. She wore her usual plain black shirt and trousers.
Instead of her leafy crown, she wore a band of silver in
her hair. She also wore an aura of glamorie, of beauty
and nobility. Rook squinted and saw, behind it, that the
Mór looked more tired than usual, her face lined and her
hair like a crest of ruffled black feathers, not shining, but
dull. Her eyes were a little too bright, and darted around
the room as if she was nervous. Seeing Rook come in,
she caught his eye and gave a tiny nod. Wait, she meant.

On a chair beside the Mór sat the Huldre, the Lady of
the people of this place. Rook knew about the Huldre.
She had her own kind of glamorie. In the daytime she
was a loathly old hag. As soon as the sun went down she
turned into the cheerful-looking young woman sitting
opposite the Mór. She had long, curly golden hair and
rosy cheeks, and wore a clinging dress made of soft white
leather trimmed with white fur, and a crown made of
holly twigs and leaves. The dress had stains down the
front from where the Huldre had spilled her dinner, and
the hem was dirty from being dragged on the ground.

Rook stood quietly by the door. His head spun and

the wolf bites on his arms and chest burned. It'd been a long day; first the ride through the Way that the Huldre had opened for them, then getting Phouka settled and persuading one of the horse grooms to re-bandage the bites. The groom hadn't done a very good job; Rook felt the bites gnaw at him with every move he made. Then the business with Fer and the wildling girl, Twig.

" . . . as soon as possible," the Huldre was saying. Her body looked as fresh as a ripe apple, but the voice was cracked and dry like an old woman's. "It is as if the land has been poisoned. Well, you are a Lady, as I am. So you feel the land, just as I do."

"Of course," the Mór said grimly.

"I do not like this way you have of bringing the spring, you know. It doesn't feel right. But winter has lasted far too long," the Huldre went on. "We can't wait any longer for spring to come, so we will do what we must."

The Mór shook her head. "I need more time," she said. "I have added somebody new to my retinue and she needs training." She hunched forward in her chair. "Her participation in the hunt will make it exceptionally powerful. And this will give you more time to find us appropriate prey. It will be an excellent hunt."

"My goodness, it will have to be, to break the hold of this terrible winter we've had," the Huldre said. "It's the worst I can remember." She rubbed her snub nose, thinking. "Leaf Woman would put things right. I wish she would return to her proper place."

"As do we all wish," the Mór said briskly. "But Leaf Woman has gone away, and we must do the best we can without her."

"Yes, I suppose we must," the Huldre said with a sigh. She moved like an old woman too, leaning on the arms of her chair to lift herself to her feet. "Take the time you need. Train this protégé of yours, and then she can spill the prey's blood and bring us our spring."

"Three days," the Mór said.

"Three days it is," the Huldre agreed with a nod. She turned and hobbled toward the door, the fur hem of her dress dragging on the rug. Seeing Rook, she stopped. "Oh!" She clapped her hands together. "It's your puck!" She stepped closer and Rook held himself still while she leaned in to examine him with nearsighted eyes. Her breath smelled like rotten teeth. She *was* beautiful, though, even to his eyes, even from up close, her skin smooth and unwrinkled, her hair shining. "He's younger than the puck you had last time, isn't he?" the Huldre asked, turning back to the Lady. "Wherever did you get him?"

The Mór leaned forward in her chair, her eyes narrowed. "He took on his puck-brother's oath," she said sharply. "He is bound to me."

The Huldre turned back to Rook with an enticing smile. "I could use a clever puck. I don't suppose you'd like to transfer your oath to me, would you, child?"

Anything would be better than being bound to the Mór. But he didn't have that choice. "It's a thrice-sworn oath," he muttered.

The Huldre stepped back, and the smile dropped off her face. "Oh," she said. "But that's—" She glanced at the Mór and then back to Rook. "I'm very sorry," she whispered. She reached out with her hand and patted his face. "Poor puck. I can do nothing to help you."

Rook stared. He'd hardly expect her to help.

One more gentle pat, and the Huldre pasted the cheerful smile back on her face, turned to nod to the Mór, and ducked out of the tent. A wisp of drumming and shouting leaked in as the tent flap was swept aside, and was muffled again when it fell.

"Hm." The Mór put her elbows on the arms of her carpet-covered chair and folded her clawlike hands under her chin. "You've been gone a long time, escorting Gwynnefar back to her tent after dinner. What has she been up to?"

"This and that," Rook muttered.

The Mór frowned. "I will make it an order if I have to, Robin. Tell me what the girl has been up to."

He hated telling her. *Hated* it. He took a deep breath. "That maid of yours, Burr," he said. "Her sister was wildling. She asked Fer for help."

"Fer?" the Mór interrupted, her eyebrows raised.

He shook his aching head. Stupid, calling her by that name in front of the Mór. "Gwynnefar," he said. "Burr took us to her sister and Gwynnefar healed her."

"How concise you are," the Mór said, her voice dry. "Tell me more. How did this healing work, exactly?"

Rook knew what she was asking. He waited a sullen moment before answering. "It's what you think," he said. "She used herbs and spells."

The Mór's face grew still and cold. "So she is a healer, is she? Like her foolish mother." Then she fell silent, perched on the edge of her chair with her shoulders hunched, staring down at the carpet beneath her feet. "She will not like to spill blood," she muttered. At last her head jerked up. "Well, it is not what I wanted to hear." Her face grew even colder. "Did you see what she did during our dinner, Robin? She sought to compel me to answer a thrice-asked question."

She'd nearly done it, too. Fer had resisted the Mór's glamorie enough to demand answers of her, and that meant she was powerful.

"She could be dangerous. But I *will* bind her to me," the Mór said fiercely. "I must have her power bound to mine. I will bind her with blood, and my power in the land will be secured."

Bound with blood. Rook knew exactly what she meant

by that. He hated it, but there was nothing he could do about it.

The Mór gave a sharp nod. "You have done very well, Robin. I think you should name a reward."

He didn't even stop to think. "I want my shifter-bone back, and the tooth." So he could be a proper puck again.

"Oh, I don't think so," the Mór said. "Not yet. Soon, maybe. In the meantime, I want you to keep watching Gwynnefar. And remember, no answering her questions."

"What if I have a question?" Rook asked. He could do what Fer had tried to do, ask once, twice, three times, and force her to tell what had really happened to the true Lady and her human lover.

The Mór jerked herself to her feet, crossed the tent, and raised her hand. Rook kept himself from flinching away. "Do you dare ask a question of me, my puck?" she asked, her voice low, threatening. "Do you dare ask it three times?" She leaned closer. "Imagine what I might do to your puck-brother if I were compelled to answer."

Rook swallowed the question down. It was too big a risk. "No," he whispered. "No question."

"I didn't think so." The Mór's bony hand patted his face, just as the Huldre had done. "You look unwell, Robin. Go and sleep."

"Oh, sure I will," Rook said. With all this going on,

was he likely to sleep? Still, he stepped toward the tent's door. As he pushed the hanging carpet aside to step out, he paused. "Have you noticed," he said nastily, "that your guards are in the last stages of wildling?"

The Mór's eyes flashed silver, sharp as needles. "Leave it, Robin. That is for me to deal with."

Without answering, he stepped outside the tent. The Huldre and her people had gone. The drums were silent and the dancers had drifted away, and somebody had thrown snow on the bonfire to put it out. The night felt icy cold and empty. Overhead the half moon marched across a flat, black sky.

Rook headed toward the tent where Phouka and the other horses were stabled. Phouka, his puck-brother, stuck in his horse form, who had gotten him into this mess in the first place. He felt shivery and light-headed. *Go sleep*, she had said. He wouldn't sleep, but he needed to lie down for a bit and not think about the way the true Lady's daughter and her questions picked at the tight bonds of his thrice-sworn oath to the Mór.

twelve

Fer woke up in the gray time before sunrise, shivering inside a cocoon of silk sheets and two coverlets. She lay still for a moment, looking up at the sloped, blue-green ceiling of the tent. Last night she'd discovered something about who she really was. In this land, she was a healer. Today she would have lessons from the Lady, and she would learn more.

Her stomach felt hollow—she was hungry for breakfast—but she was nervous, too. Lessons with Grand-Jane meant reading dusty herb lore and cleaning the stillroom and making up tinctures and lotions and electuaries. Boring, often enough. Warrior lessons with the Lady would not, Fer felt sure, be boring.

They might even be dangerous.

Steeling herself against the ice-cold air, Fer unwrapped herself from the coverlets, leaped out of bed, and flung on her jeans, woolen socks and sneakers, two T-shirts, her sweater, and, on top of it all, her patch-jacket. With cold fingers she braided her hair, sticking the Lady's black feather in the rubber band at the end of the braid.

On the chest she found a tray with breakfast on it; somebody must have brought it in while she slept. Also on the tray was a bottle stoppered with a cork and sealed with wax. Fer ran her finger over the seal. The wax came from Grand-Jane's beehives. This was a message from her grandma, sent through the Way. Somebody— she wondered who—had brought it from the Way and left it for her to find.

Opening the bottle, Fer pulled out the letter rolled up inside and read it.

Jennifer—
Things here have gotten very bad.
My girl, when you opened the Way, something happened. It has been weeks since you left, and spring has still not come. The rains continue, every day. Winter has been creeping back in. The river through town is flooding, and none of the farmers have been able to put in their crops.
I am afraid that something from that world is

spilling over into ours.
You must come home at once. I need you here.

Fer jumped to her feet. Grand-Jane needed her!

But wait. She couldn't come at once. For one thing, she wasn't sure, exactly, where she was. They'd ridden through the sky, or through another Way to get here, and she didn't know how to get back.

Her heart gave a thump. Grand-Jane was right, though. Something *was* wrong in this land. The wildling was evidence of that, and so was the stag hunt, and the over-long winter, and the Lady's strange, twisty answers to Fer's questions. And if the wrongness here was spilling over into her own world, it was her fault. She was the one who had opened the Way.

"That means I have to close it," Fer whispered to herself. But how? Rook couldn't tell her. The Lady wouldn't tell her, she felt sure.

If she couldn't close the Way, she'd have to set right whatever was wrong here. Spring hadn't come there, Grand-Jane had written. The Lady brought the spring, Rook had told her. Maybe if the Lady brought the spring to all the lands, spring would come at home, too.

She would stay, she decided. Stay until she figured out what was wrong and then help to fix it.

That decided, she sat down on her camp bed and ate her breakfast and drank the cooling tea.

While eating, she eyed the other thing she'd found on the chest. A warm-looking coat, black wool like the one Rook wore, but with a hood and silky-soft black fur at the collar and cuffs. She was supposed to wear it instead of her patch-jacket, she knew. But to trade her jacket for the Lady's gift would be to leave Grand-Jane's protection, and she wasn't willing to do that.

She waited a bit longer for Burr or Rook to fetch her for her lessons with the Lady. But they didn't come. Fer stuck her head out of the tent flap. A black crow was perched on one of the bent birch trees nearby, waiting for her. The sky was cloudy gray, the pine trees dark, as if night was still clinging to them. The air smelled of fresh pine needles and of wood smoke. The camp was stirring, the Lady's people like shadows in the gray light, coming and going.

Fer stepped outside, then paused and closed her eyes.

At first she just heard the breeze sighing in the pine branches overhead, and then she reached out to the land all around her. It was frozen and dead. In the distance, she sensed, the land rose up into mountains, and winter gripped them, too, even colder than here. Under her feet, she felt roots trapped in the frozen ground, felt how they longed to stretch and send tendrils toward a warmer sun.

She opened her eyes, wondering. At home she had felt the spring coming, the change in the air and in the swelling in the tree buds, but that was nothing to how connected she felt to this land. It was like . . . almost like she had extra senses, or like the land was part of her. It was like magic. No, it *was* magic.

Taking a deep breath, Fer headed down the snowy path. A pile of charred wood lay in the middle of a trampled-down space before the Lady's tent. She'd heard the sound of dancing and drumming last night, but she'd been too tired to see what it was. Some kind of feast, maybe, with a bonfire.

Seeing her coming, a gray-clad wolf-guard, the female one, came to meet her.

"Quick word in your ear, healer-girl?" the she-wolf said. Her words came out on puffs of steam in the icy cold air.

"Okay," Fer said, stopping. She shoved her hands into her jacket pockets. "What do you want?"

"It's like this." The she-wolf stepped closer. "We need your help."

Fer nodded. "All right. Help with what?"

Across the cleared space, the Lady ducked under her tent flap and stepped outside.

"Ah, nothing," the wolf-guard said, seeing the Lady. "Never mind. No need to mention it." She trotted ahead and, with a quick bow to the Lady, went to stand beside the tent.

Fer followed, more slowly.

The Lady stood slim and tall, beautiful from the top of her black hair to the soles of her black deerskin boots. "Good morning, Gwynnefar." Her eyes narrowed, disapproving. "Did you not receive the coat I sent for you?"

"I got it," Fer said. She shrugged her shoulders inside her patch-jacket. "Thanks, but this one's warm enough."

For just a second the Lady looked angry, but then her face smoothed into a smile. "Are you ready?"

Fer nodded, still thinking about her connection to the land. "Can you feel the land here?" she asked.

The Lady's eyes narrowed. "Feel the land? What do you mean?"

"It's hard to describe it," Fer answered. "I can feel the ground and the sky and the trees." She turned and pointed out of the forest. "I know there are mountains that way, and that it's going to storm there in not too long. And I can feel that there's something wrong here."

The Lady had gone very pale. "Ah, yes," she said quickly. "Of course I can feel the land. I am a Lady of the land; of course I can. I feel it far more strongly than you do."

Oh. Fer pushed on to her next question, even though she knew the Lady wasn't going to like it. "How do you bring the spring to the land?" she asked.

The Lady gazed down at Fer, her beautiful face still, like stone. "Ah," she said at last. "I am glad you asked that question. I bring the spring through a kind of ritual. You will learn more about it soon. It will be one of your lessons."

Fer opened her mouth to ask about the open Way, and to tell her about how spring wasn't coming at her home.

But the Lady interrupted. "Do not ask me any more questions, Gwynnefar. I find it wearying." She turned the force of her glamorie onto Fer. "Do you understand?"

Fer clutched the spell-bag in her jacket pocket and blinked, and the power of the glamorie faded. No, she didn't understand. But before she could protest, the Lady turned away and led Fer from the tents among the trees and out to the field beyond, where Fer and Rook had landed at the end of the wild ride. Waiting for them in the field were two badger-men, bundled up to their chins in warm coats and scarves, each holding a horse. The marble-white one for the Lady, and Phouka, tossing his mane, for Fer. The badger-men handed over the horses, bowed, and left.

"Mount up," the Lady ordered.

"Okay," Fer said. Beside her, Phouka stood quietly, knee-deep in snow. His yellow-gold eyes watched her closely. She reached out with a careful hand and patted his nose. He snorted.

She didn't have Rook here to give her a leg up, but

she thought she could do it without his help. With her left hand she grabbed Phouka's mane, then she backed away, took a running step, jumped, and pulled herself up at the same time.

As she swung up, Phouka took a half step sideways, and Fer slid right over the top of his back, and then— *phlump!*—she was facedown in the snow on his other side.

"And again," the Lady said. When *she* had mounted up, she had looked graceful.

Fer stood up and brushed snow off her jacket. Right, try again. This time, when Phouka tried his side-step trick, Fer was ready for it. She jumped, belly-flopped onto his back, then, clinging to his mane, scrambled around until she had her legs on either side.

For the rest of the morning, in the snow-covered field, the Lady taught Fer to sit straight and tall, to turn the horse by shifting her weight slightly and pressing her outside leg against his side, and to trot without bouncing. Sometimes Phouka did as he was told, and sometimes he didn't. At first she felt like a bag of potatoes bouncing around on Phouka's back, and her bottom got sore. She knew she looked nothing like the Lady, who rode with smooth grace, as if she was one with her horse.

Fer fell off twice, and she was sure that Phouka was laughing at her as she got to her feet covered with snow.

He snorted, anyway, and tossed his head both times it happened. But after a while, Fer started to feel the rhythm of riding. She'd be going along, *jolt-jolt-jolt*, and then, just like on the wild ride, the bumping would turn to rocking and she'd find her balance, and lean with Phouka as he turned, and move with his motion. It was like flying, but better, faster.

After a quick lunch, they went back to the field with Phouka and the Lady's white horse. Fat flakes of snow were drifting down from the sky. Crows perched in the pine trees at the edge of the field, watching.

The Lady led Fer and Phouka across the field and onto a trail through the pine forest, going away from the encampment. The forest was silent except for the *shuff-shuff* of hooves in snow and the *shush* of wind high up in the tops of the trees.

Ahead of her, the Lady whispered to her horse and it stopped, then fell in beside Phouka. "I want more than anything to win you to my side, Gwynnefar," she said.

To her side? "I'm not against you, um, Lady," Fer said.

The Lady tilted her head, birdlike. "Yet I think you suspect me of things, terrible things." She smiled, and this time Fer saw the icy net of the glamorie as it dropped over her. This time it was cold, like metal bars, like being caged.

This had to be wrong. The Lady used the magic of

the glamorie to force her people to obey her. Fer stared down at Phouka's tangled black mane. She took a deep breath, fighting against the glamorie as it forced her mind away from her questions and doubts. She had meant to ask the Lady about the wrongness she felt here, about the wildling. And to ask her why Rook was bound to her so tightly, even though he hated it. She wouldn't get answers from this Lady, she was sure of that now. "I don't suspect you," she said slowly. But maybe, she realized, she should. The thought made her feel icy cold and shaky inside.

The Lady didn't answer. After a moment, as if nothing had happened, she said, "We must continue with your lessons, Gwynnefar." She pointed ahead at a log, an old tree that had fallen across the path. "You are going to jump that."

Fer shivered, still thinking about her new suspicions of the Lady. Then she blinked and examined the log the Lady was still pointing to. Better go along with her for now. Hmm. The log didn't look *too* high. "C'mon, Phouka," she said, squeezing her legs to tell him to go forward. "Let's go take a look at it first."

After Phouka had snuffled at the log for a bit, Fer brought him back down the path where the Lady waited.

"Horses cannot judge distance very well," the Lady said. "But Phouka knows what he's doing. When he begins the jump, lift your seat, move your hands forward to give him room, and lean over the crest of his neck. It's a matter of balance and timing."

Fer nodded, the instructions whirling around in her head. She squeezed her legs. "Go, Phouka," she told him. They jolted off down the path, then Fer found the rhythm. As they came up to the log, she felt Phouka gather himself; his muscles bunched and his front legs came off the ground, and then his back legs. His back arched, and Fer leaned forward, finding her balance. As he landed, he lowered his head, and *whoosh*, she was tumbling over his shoulder, landing facedown in the deep snow.

She sat up, wiping snow out of her eyes. Phouka trotted a few more steps, then turned and came back, snorting and giving her a wicked glance with his yellow eyes.

Was he laughing at her again?

She got to her feet and led him over to the log, which she used to climb onto his back, then rode down the path where the Lady was waiting.

"Again," she said.

Fer fell off four more times. The fourth time, she sat up in the snow, grinning. "Phouka, you did that on purpose," she said, wiping snow out of her face. Phouka lowered his head and tossed his mane, then stepped forward and pushed his nose against her shoulder. She climbed to her feet. "You bad horse," she said, and patted his neck.

The Lady came up, very tall and dark against the graywhite sky. She was frowning. "You don't carry the whip I gave you, Gwynnefar," she said. "He'd behave better if you reminded him now and then that he is bound to serve you."

Bound to her? That was a strange way to talk about a horse. Fer leaned her head against Phouka's neck. "I will *never* use a whip on you," she whispered into his ear. He couldn't understand her, she knew, but she felt better telling him. She patted him again, and he whuffled his nose against her shoulder.

The Lady decided Fer had learned enough about horses for one day. They rode through the falling snow, back to the encampment, where the Lady left Fer at her tent. "You'll be tired," the Lady said, almost like she was giving Fer an order. She handed her horse over to one of the badger-men. "Go straight to bed. I must go out of the encampment to meet with someone, so I will have dinner sent to you."

Fer slid down from Phouka's back. When her feet hit the snowy ground, all the soreness of strained muscles from her first day of riding hit her at once. "Ooh," she breathed. She patted Phouka to say good-bye, then turned to the Lady, who stood with the snow falling around her and her eyes gleaming as if they were full of stars.

"Good night, Gwynnefar," the Lady said. Her voice sounded like silvery music.

"Good night," Fer said slowly. She turned her head, to see if she could catch a glimpse of what was behind the Lady's glamorie.

Before she saw anything, the Lady turned and strode away. Fer blinked. Bed. She was going to flop on her bed and not move until morning. She ducked stiffly under the flap and hobbled into her tent.

Gingerly she eased herself down onto her bed. Ooh, the muscles in her legs hurt. And her bottom felt like one big bruise. She bent down to untie her sneakers.

Then she stopped. The Lady had gone off to meet someone, she'd said. Rook was somewhere else, not spying on her. Now was the perfect time to do some spying of her own.

thirteen

Fer's patch-jacket was lined on the inside with dark brown calico. She took the jacket off and turned it inside out and put it on again. She'd be harder to see that way, as she snuck through the encampment.

She went to the tent flap and peeked out. Evening was coming on, but nobody had lit the lanterns that hung from the pine trees. The snowy paths leading from tent to tent were empty. Maybe all the Lady's people and her crows had gone with her.

Keeping an eye out for the wolf-guards, Fer went down the path, past one dark tent, past another, past a snow-covered pine tree and another tent that had light leaking out from under its tent-flap doorway. She paused outside the flap, listening. A wind rustled the pine branches, far overhead, but everything else was quiet.

She turned to continue down the path, toward the Lady's tent, when she saw a dark shape coming closer. She froze. The she-wolf guard, looking grim and gray and fierce in the gloomy light.

Uh-oh. Fer gulped. She'd tell the guard that she was . . . hungry, that she'd come out of her tent to find some food.

Fer opened her mouth to start explaining, but the she-wolf looked straight at Fer and her face didn't change; her eyes just slid away and she passed Fer, her heavy feet going *crunch-crunch-crunch* on the snowy path.

Fer stared after her. Had the wolf-guard not seen her? She looked down at herself. The brown lining of the patch-jacket made her blend in a little with the night, but she wasn't invisible. Was she?

Fer stepped back onto the path and headed toward the Mór's tent. She walked a few steps and stopped, listening.

Again somebody was coming, this time from behind her. Fer stepped off the path and looked back. One of the Lady's people, a badger-man carrying a torch. His broad face seemed orange in the dancing light. He came closer and Fer hunched down into her patch-jacket. He passed by without even glancing aside at her.

Fer let out a breath she hadn't realized she'd been holding. She *was* invisible! Maybe Grand-Jane's patch-jacket had more power here than it did back home. Feeling more confident, she went along the path until she reached the Lady's tent. A wolf-guard stood out front, doing his job. Guarding. A glowing lantern sat in the snow nearby.

Fer paused. She might as well try it. Keeping her feet quiet on the path, Fer crept closer to the tent flap, watching the guard's face. He looked out into the night, showing no sign of seeing or hearing her as she edged past him. She ducked under the flap and into the Lady's tent.

She straightened, her heart jumping with excitement, and looked around. The tent looked just as it had when she'd eaten dinner here. Summer-green carpets on the floor and hanging from the walls. A table and chairs and a camp bed just like the one in her own tent. A lantern turned low sat on the table. And, against one tent wall, a wooden chest. That was the place to look for clues about what was wrong here.

Her feet silent on the carpeted floor, Fer crossed the tent and opened the chest. It was full mostly of shirts and trousers, all made of black silk. Among the neatly folded clothes, Fer found a box. It was made of the same light-colored wood as her OWEN box, but a little bigger. Fer took the box over to the table where the lantern was so she'd be able to see better. She opened the box.

She found three things inside. The first was a bunch of glossy black feathers tied together with thread. Fer gave them a quick glance and set them aside, pulling out the next thing. It was yet another box made of the same wood, but smaller, only the size of her fist. It rattled when she gave it a shake. Inside the little box were two lumps of something. Fer dumped them out into her hand and held them up to the lantern to see them better. One was smooth and pointed like a sharp tooth. Yes, it was a fang from a dog or a wolf. The other thing looked like a chunk of bone. They were both about the size of the end of her pinkie finger. Fer put them back in the box and examined the last thing.

It was circle shaped and lumpy, wrapped in a piece of sky-blue silk. Fer unwrapped it and turned it in her hands. The crown the Lady had been wearing during the wild ride. It was a circlet made of living twigs and budding oak leaves, green and glowing with the magic of the land, even here in the darkness of winter. Fer held it closer to see it more clearly.

No, wait. The crown wasn't as green and healthy as it had first appeared in the dim light. The leaves looked freshly budded, but they were limp and edged with the dry brown of autumn. Spots of black mold marred their surface. A smell like rotting flowers hung in the air. The twigs felt slimy under her fingers. Fer set it down with shaking hands.

It was the Lady's crown, and it was dying.

fourteen

The dying crown meant that the wrongness Fer felt in the land had to have something to do with the Lady.

But the Lady had told Fer herself—the Lady could feel the land. The Lady was *bound* to the land and her people, just as much as any of her people were bound to her by their oaths. She must have done something terrible, Fer realized. Something that made her own people turn wildling and made this feeling of wrongness seep through the land.

Fer needed to talk to Rook. He couldn't know about the dying crown, and he needed to know about it. Maybe once he knew that the Lady was evil, he would be free of her, and he could explain how things were supposed to work here, to help her figure out how to fix what was wrong. After putting everything carefully away, she slipped back outside and to her own tent. All night long, the questions and thoughts whirled in her head.

In the morning, Rook didn't bring Fer's breakfast. Instead it was Burr who crept in with a tray full of bread and hot tea.

"Have you seen Rook?" Fer asked. She'd gulped down two slices of bread and honey, even though she still felt sick and shaky from what she'd found the night before.

Burr pushed her shoulder, making her sit on the bed so she could braid her hair. "The puck is hers," Burr said.

Fer gritted her teeth. "I know that. I have to talk to him. Have you seen him?"

"No," Burr said. With quick fingers, she finished the braid and tucked the Lady's black feather into its end.

Fer turned to face her. Time for a question. "Burr, something is wrong in this land, isn't it. Do you know what it is?"

Burr's eyes widened.

Through her connection to the other girl, Fer felt how her heart trembled at Fer's question.

"We are bound to her," Burr whispered, her voice shaky. "We are all winterlings, cold and alone. Spring will never come for us. We are not to speak of it."

"But you *know*, don't you?" Fer insisted. "Something happened. The Lady did something terrible."

"I can't answer," Burr said. Fer felt the girl shivering. "Find Leaf Woman. Ask her. She is not bound. She can tell." Tears welled up in her eyes, and she ducked her head and scurried out of the tent.

Leaf Woman again. What did *she* have to do with it all?

With a sigh, Fer put her head into her hands. She was a girl, and she was alone, and she didn't have any power. The Lady was a strong warrior with the glamorie and the power of the land behind her. For a moment, Fer felt like giving up, like fleeing back through the Way to the safety of Grand-Jane's house.

But no. The wrongness from this land was seeping into her own world too, Grand-Jane's letter had said. And she couldn't leave this land stained and shadowed as it was. She had to do something. Her own father had gone back through the Way to help her mother put things right. He'd been a human, alone in a land of magic and danger, and he'd done it. They must have tried to stop the Lady from doing whatever evil thing she'd done. They'd both failed, she could see that.

Fer stood up and gave a firm nod. She would find out what the Lady had done to bring wrongness to the land, and she would set it right

Until she found the answer and fixed what was wrong, she couldn't go home to Grand-Jane. But she could send her a letter about it.

Fer dug her pencil and paper out of her backpack and wrote a note.

Dear Grand-Jane,

You are right that something wrong here is coming through the Way to mess things up there. I'm sure it's because of something the Lady did, but I don't know what. I can feel spring here, wanting to come, but the winter is staying longer than it should. People here are wildling and I think they might be turning wild because they're sworn to serve a Lady who has gone bad. Does that sound right to you? I found her crown, and it's dying.

The Lady is very beautiful, and she makes things hard to think about. She says my mother was her most trusted ally and warrior, and that I should serve her as my mother did. At first I thought I would serve her, but now I know that I can't do that.

My father brought me to you, and then he came back here to help my mother put things right. But they didn't. I think I'm supposed to do it instead, and I will, once I find out what, exactly, is wrong, and how I can fix it.

I haven't forgotten my oath to you. I will come home. But I can't come yet.

Love,
Fer

After signing the letter, Fer stuffed it in the bottle and sealed it with the cork and left it on the tray. Hopefully the same person who had left Grand-Jane's note would take her note back to the Way and send it.

Now she had another day of lessons with the Lady while trying to fight off the glamorie without letting any of her doubts show. Instead she would have to watch the Lady closely, to see if she could discover any clues about what she had done to bring wrongness to the land.

And meanwhile, *where* was Rook? If he was supposed to be watching her for the Lady, he wasn't doing a very good job.

The Lady greeted Fer with a cold kiss on her forehead, and she looked just the same, glowing with beauty and power. But now that she knew that the wrongness in the land came from the Lady who should be the land's defender, Fer felt herself resist the glamorie as it dropped over her. Just to see what would happen, Fer tried turning her head to catch a glimpse of the Lady out of the corner of her eye—to see what was really there, behind the glamorie.

But she stumbled over a log hidden in the snow and saw only the Lady's chilly, pale face.

Fer and the Lady trudged through the knee-high snow to the field, where two badger-men held the horses. Fer felt her heart lift when she saw Phouka. Leaving the Lady, she ran up to him and patted his flank. "Hello, you bad horse," she said, and laid her cheek against his neck. He smelled of hay and warmth and earth. He whuffled and turned to rub his nose against her shoulder.

The Lady swung up onto her horse's back. "Mount up, Gwynnefar," she ordered.

"Be good, Phouka," Fer whispered into his ear, then gripped his mane and did her belly-flop mount. She scrambled into a sitting position.

"We will ride for a short while today," the Lady said, "and then I will teach you to shoot the bow and arrow." Then she dug her heels into her horse's side and trotted off into the snowy field.

Fer followed. Overhead the sky was clear and light blue, and a chilly wind blew, making the tips of Fer's ears and her bare fingers burn with cold. Her breath huffed out as clouds of steam. As always, her patch-jacket kept her warm. She bounced after the Lady. After an hour of riding, the Lady led them out of the forest to the wide field. At its other end, Fer could see the encampment, the blue and green and violet-purple tents clustered under the eaves of the forest, smudges of gray smoke drifting from the campfires, a few glimpses of the Lady's people coming and going between the trees.

Fer had a question that she had to ask, even though she didn't trust the Lady to tell the truth about anything. Might as well risk it. "Lady," she asked, "I haven't seen

Rook in days. Do you know where he is?"

"He is probably sulking," the Lady answered. "His kind is terribly moody."

"What is his kind?" Fer asked. She knew what Grand-Jane had told her about pucks, but she was curious about what the Lady would tell her.

"The pucks? They are different from all the others of our kind. Pucks have very keen vision, for one thing, and are valued for that. They are tricksy and not to be trusted unless they are carefully bound by an oath of loyalty. Also, they can shift into other animals. Horse and dog. Some can shift into a goat, as well."

"How does a puck do the shifting?" she asked, since the Lady was in a strangely answering mood.

The Lady cast her a sharp, sidelong glance. "The pucks use an animal bone or a tooth to shift."

Fer had found a dog tooth in the box in the Lady's tent, and a bit of bone. She hadn't seen another puck in the camp, so it must be Rook's, the tooth he used to shift into a dog, and a bone for a horse. Why did the Lady have them?

"When a puck is a horse or a dog," the Lady said, "he is not a mindless wildling, he can still think and remember and act with intelligence. Usually the pucks serve no one. However, they can, in very rare cases, be oath-bound, and a bound puck is beyond value."

Fer asked the next question without thinking. "What would happen if a puck broke his oath?"

The Lady pulled her horse to a stop. Phouka walked on a few steps, then stopped, and Fer turned him back. The Lady's face was pale and tight. "What has he told you?" she asked.

"He won't tell me anything," Fer answered. Her heart gave a little lurch. "I just wondered."

"Ah." The Lady fell silent. When she spoke the edge had left her voice. She almost sounded sad. "Our oaths and our rules bind us together, Gwynnefar. When an oath is broken there is a price. And it is always more than the oath breaker can pay."

fifteen

Before Fer could ask any more questions, the Lady and her horse galloped ahead to the waiting badger-men, where she dismounted and took the two bows and quivers of arrows they were holding. Fer followed, sliding down from Phouka's back.

"See you later," she whispered, giving him a pat as one of the badger-men led him away.

For the rest of the morning, the Lady taught Fer how to shoot with the bow and arrow. She set up a target on a pine tree and, after strapping a leather guard onto Fer's left wrist, had Fer stand in the snow twenty paces away. She taught her to raise the bow, aim, and shoot. The Lady could hit the target every time, her arrows flying straight and true.

Fer's arrows splattered and splayed around the target,

but after a few hours of the Lady's teaching, Fer raised the bow, drew back the string, sighted along the arrow, and felt something settle into rightness inside her. Even before she released the string, she knew the arrow would find the target. She nodded, hearing the *thunk* as it hit, dead center.

"Well done," the Lady said. "Someday you will be as skilled with the bow as your mother was."

Fer gulped. But her mother's bow had shot down her father by mistake. That's what the Lady had said. She looked down at the bow in her hands, the smooth, curving wood, the taut string. Did she even *want* to be a warrior?

"I have some business to see to," the Lady said, interrupting Fer's thoughts. "I am meeting with the Huldre. Practice by yourself for another hour." She stared down at Fer for a moment, her face cold. "Tomorrow you will face a test to see if you've earned a place by my side." Then she left Fer, striding away toward the camp.

Fer gulped. A test? That sounded bad. The Lady's certainty that Fer would serve her as a warrior made her feel shaky inside, but Fer went on practicing, feeling the rightness a few more times. She sighted down the arrow and sent it straight into the target, *thunk*. Then she tramped through the snow and yanked the arrow out, holding it in her hand.

Then she closed her eyes. She could feel the land

beneath her feet and all around her, and she could feel the stain on the land, like a shadow over the sky, almost like a bitter taste in her mouth. It was wrong, all wrong.

The Lady felt this too, she said. But how could she, if she was the one who had caused it?

Hearing footsteps in the snow, Fer opened her eyes. One of the wolf-guards.

"Hey-ho, healer-girl," the wolf-guard said. It was the female, the tallest of the three guards.

"Hi." Shutting away her awareness of the land, Fer examined the fingers of her right hand. The skin was blistered from holding the string of the bow and pulling it back. And her shoulders felt heavy and stiff. Time to stop and find something to eat.

"It's like this," the wolf-guard said, walking beside Fer as she headed back toward the encampment. "We hear you're a healer and like to help people and you have good magic."

Fer shrugged and stuck an arrow into the quiver slung over her shoulder. She wasn't really a healer, at least she didn't think she was, but it'd be too hard to explain everything to the wolf-woman. "What's wrong?" she asked, though she could guess the answer already.

The wolf-guard stepped closer. Fer looked up into her worried face, at her grizzled gray hair and heavy eyebrows and yellowing teeth. A thread of connection tied them together; Fer felt it, just like her connection with Twig and Burr. She had to help.

"We're wildling," the wolf-woman said.

"I'll get my stuff," Fer said.

After stopping at her own tent for her backpack and the OWEN box, Fer followed the woman wolf-guard to her tent. They ducked inside.

Fer heard growling and blinked until her eyes adjusted to the dimness. One of the wolf-guards still looked like a person; the other still was a person, but was crouched on all fours, snarling, long ropes of drool hanging from his slavering jaws. The other guard gripped his shirt collar, holding him back so he wouldn't leap at Fer and tear her throat out. Wildling for sure.

"I'll mix up the herbs to make the medicine," Fer said, turning to the wolf-woman. "But *you* are giving it to him."

When she'd finished mixing the herbs and saying the spell, and they'd managed to get some of the honeyed paste into the wildest of the three wolves, saving some for the other two, Fer checked them through the seeing-stone.

"You'll be okay," she said, putting the stone into the OWEN box. "But he"—she pointed at the wildest—"might need another dose. Let me know if he does." When she'd healed the two wolf-guards of their wilding, she'd felt her connection to them spin out strong, like a bow string drawn taut. It was a strange feeling, sensing how their hearts beat, how they feared the way they lost themselves in the wildling. Knowing that they looked at her and saw . . . not a girl, but something else. She wasn't sure what.

"You did us a favor, healer-girl," the female wolf-guard said. "You going to take our oaths?"

"No," Fer said. She was starting to get tired of promises and oaths.

"Yep, that's what we heard," the she-wolf said. "So now we do you a favor." Her partner nodded.

"All right," Fer said. She closed the OWEN box and stuffed it into her backpack. "Here's a good favor. You can tell me where Rook is." She got creakily to her feet and slung her backpack over her shoulder.

"The puck is sick," the she-wolf said.

The other wolf-guard pushed her. "Shhh, don't tell her that."

The she-wolf pushed back. "No, the healer-girl likes the puck. And we owe her a favor, you said."

"If Rook is sick," Fer put in, her stomach giving a sudden twist of worry, "you'd better take me to him."

"Righty-oh!" The shorter guard turned to Fer and bared his teeth.

Fer blinked and stepped back. Oh. He was smiling.

A very wolfish smile.

The wolf-guards led her away from the tents, through the forest on a wider track trodden through the snow to a tent pitched in the middle of a clearing. Unlike the Lady's tents, this one was made of stained canvas. Piles of hay were stacked on either side of the wide-open door at one end, and on the other side of the tent was a pile of old straw and manure. Pulled up next to it were the two wagons used to transport all the gear during the wild ride.

The tent was the stable for the horses and the deer and goats who served as mounts to the Lady's people. Another, smaller tent must be for the animals' grooms, the badger-men.

The tent had a dirt floor and a long central aisle interrupted by tall poles, and it had canvas walls strung up on wires to make separate stalls for the mounts. Fer followed the wolf-guards to the end of the tent farthest from the open door; one of the guards pulled a flap aside to reveal a stall. Not much light reached this end of the tent from the door; the stall was dark. Fer saw shifting shadows.

Then Phouka poked out his nose and snorted.

Fer reached out to pat his neck, but he shifted back and stood stiff-legged across the stall, his head up and ears laid back. He was blocking her way in.

"Rook's in here?" Fer asked.

Both wolf-guards nodded.

She stepped into the stall, peering into the shadows behind Phouka. Curled into the corner, his back against a tent pole, was Rook. His eyes were closed. "Rook?" she whispered, taking a step forward.

Phouka snorted again and stamped a hoof, but didn't move out of the way. He was protecting Rook.

Fer reached up a careful hand and laid it against Phouka's nose. "I'm just going to help him," she said. Phouka pushed against her hand, then shook his head.

Taking that for wary acceptance, Fer ducked past the horse and crouched next to Rook. He lay on a pile of hay, hunched into his coat. He shivered, as if he was cold, but his face was flushed. She leaned over and, brushing his shaggy hair out of the way, rested her lips on his forehead to check his temperature. Hot.

His eyes flickered open. "Oh, not you," he muttered. "Go 'way."

"Rook, you're sick," she said, her heart pounding. The Lady had said that pucks didn't turn wildling like her other people, but she had to be sure. Opening her backpack, she pulled out the OWEN box and took from it the seeing-stone. It showed the same Rook she'd seen before. Because the horse was leaning over her shoulder to poke his nose into what she was doing, she turned and looked at him through the seeing-stone too. She saw a horse, but behind the animal was a young man with long black hair and yellow-gold eyes. The young man looked an awful lot like Rook, but older. She lowered the stone. Phouka was a puck, just like Rook. But why was he a horse and never a person?

Setting the seeing-stone aside, she dug in the box. Rook's fever was from his wolf bites, which must have gotten infected. He could easily die. Even so, her herbs and spells had been working so magically well here, for sure she'd be able to heal him.

But no. She peered into one herb bag after another. All empty. The vials of tincture were all used up too. All she had left was a bit of valerian root and a few table-spoons of honey. Not enough to help much. She gulped down a knot of worry. It was winter here; nothing was growing in the snow-covered forest, so she couldn't go search for wild herbs.

Oh no, wait. She felt in her jacket pocket for the bag of herbs, the protective spell Grand-Jane had made her. And the sprig of lavender. Carefully she picked apart the stitches and opened the bag. Taking a clean T-shirt out of her backpack, she spread it on the ground, then spilled the herbs onto the cloth. More lavender, good. And mugwort and loosestrife, which would be good both in a poultice and in a tea infusion.

Tea first so he'd keep still for the poultice. Phouka poked his nose over her shoulder again. She pushed him aside. The wolf-guards were lurking by the flaps that served as the stall's door. "I need some hot water," Fer said. "Boiling hot." And to the other guard, "And some butter, if you can find any."

The taller guard tapped her nose and sketched a bow, then left, followed by the other guard.

"Why does she want butter?" Fer heard the first guard ask.

"Dunno," answered the other. "Maybe we're going to have toast."

Then they were gone.

Phouka shifted, and Fer felt his breath tickling the back of her neck. She sorted the mugwort from the loosestrife. The puck-horse nudged her shoulder. "Don't worry, Phouka," she said. "He's going to be all right." She hoped he would, anyway. Rook had been stubborn and stupid, trying to deal with the wolf bites on his own, and now they were infected and they'd be a lot harder to heal.

Carefully she took the sprig of lavender from her pocket and laid it alongside the other herbs. Too bad she didn't have any dried willow bark left. That would've helped with the fever. From her backpack she took the stone she'd been using as a mortar and crushed the mugwort and loosestrife together, adding a few of the lavender flowers.

A shuffling at the door, and Fer looked up to see the

she-wolf guard hunched over a steaming cup, almost like she was protecting it.

"Put it here," Fer said, pointing at the ground beside her. The guard edged past Phouka, set down the cup, and then headed for the door. "Don't go anywhere," Fer said while picking a few more tiny lavender flowers off the sprig and adding them to the cup. She'd need the guards' help to get Rook to drink the tea.

She stirred the crushed herbs into the hot water and added a little honey, only a very little for sweetening, because she'd need the rest for the poultice. While waiting for the herbs to infuse, she closed her eyes and whispered over the cup the healing spell Grand-Jane had taught her, the one that called on the essence of the herbs. She saw the garden, and the bees, and Grand-Jane with her big floppy hat and canvas gloves cutting the herbs, laying them out on drying racks, then sorting them into cloth bags. "By the fields of lavender," she whispered, as Grand-Jane had taught her, "by the valerian root, by the steadiness of mugwort artemisia and by loosestrife, also called lythrum salicaria, tall and bold."

There. It was ready. When she opened her eyes, the other guard stepped into the stall and bent to hand Fer a lump of butter wrapped in wilted leaves. Broad burdock leaves, Fer was glad to see. If any of their merit had gotten into the butter, her poultice would be even more effective.

Setting the butter aside, Fer picked up the cooling tea and nodded to the wolf-guards. "Sit him up for me," she ordered.

Both guards barged into the stall, setting Phouka to stamping and snorting again. One of the guards seized Rook's arms, the other a leg, and they started to drag him out of the corner he was huddled in.

"Gently!" Fer said. Stupid wolves!

The guards cowered. "Sorry," one said, and, "Sorry," the other echoed. Moving very slowly, keeping an eye on Fer, they eased Rook up, holding him by the shoulders.

Rook opened his eyes and, seeing the guards, started to struggle. "Wolves!" he gasped.

Fer grabbed his chin and made him look at her. His eyes were wide. "Rook, stop it," she said. "I'm just trying to help."

He blinked and focused on her. "Oh, it's you." He frowned. "Weren't you here before?"

"I'm still here," Fer said. She raised the cup to his lips. "Drink this, all right?" She expected a fight, but, his fever-bright eyes fixed on hers, Rook drank down the tea.

"Okay, put him down again," Fer said, and turned to look over her poultice ingredients.

"He's all sleepy," a guard said as they lowered Rook back onto his bed of hay.

"That's good," Fer said. She glanced at Rook, who lay with his eyes closed, one arm flung out. The valerian root. It must have been stronger than she'd realized, even the tiny amount she'd had left. "Get his coat and shirt off," she ordered.

While the wolf-guards obeyed, she made up a poultice, ignoring the wolf-guards' comments about toast when she added the butter and the honey. After mixing it she recited the nine-herbs charm—*mugwort, betony, lamb's cress, plaintain, mayweed, nettle, crab-apple, thyme, fennel*—once in each of Rook's ears, the way Grand-Jane had taught her, and once over the poultice. She didn't *have* the nine herbs, but the charm should still have power. When the poultice was ready, she applied it to the festering bites that slashed across Rook's chest and arms, then wrapped up the wounds with strips of her T-shirt.

"How'd he get those bites?" the she-wolf guard asked. They were both hovering by the stall door.

"They look like wolf bites," the other guard said.

Fer rolled her eyes. *Stupid* wolves. "That's what they are," she said. She packed up her things, wiped a smudge of honey off her fingers, and got to her feet. Phouka rested his head on her shoulder and they both stood looking down at Rook, who lay sleeping peacefully.

"You keep an eye on him, okay, Phouka?" she whispered.

The horse snorted, his breath warm on her neck.

She couldn't stay and watch over Rook. Anyway, he wouldn't want her to be there when he woke up. It wasn't just the valerian that had extra power here. All the herbs did, and the healing spells, and so did she. She'd always hated learning herb lore and spells, but those things, she realized, had real magic in them. She really *was* a healer, just like Grand-Jane.

And that meant she'd just saved Rook's life. For the third time.

sixteen

The next morning, as the dawn turned the darkness in her tent to dusty gray, Fer sat on the edge of her camp bed and reread the note in her hand.

Another note from her grandma, this one left in its wax-sealed bottle on the floor beside her bed. She'd found it when she'd woken up.

Jennifer, you must come home at once. If the Lady has polluted the land somehow, then you are in terrible danger from her. She is absolutely not to be trusted. Any wrongness there can be traced to whatever evil she has done, and it is not something you can fix. You must come through the Way and close it behind you, keeping the wrongness on the other side.

The flooding and storms here have gotten even worse,

and they are spreading beyond just near the Way.
Come home now, Jennifer.

—Grand-Jane

Reading the note over again, Fer shook her head. Did Grand-Jane know what she was asking? Fer couldn't leave the troubles here and just slam the Way closed behind her and then forget it all. She couldn't leave Rook bound to the Lady, or the wolf-guards in their wildling, or frightened Burr and Twig, or her dear, bad Phouka. She couldn't leave the land to suffer under the Lady.

The over-long winter here and the storms at home were caused by something the Lady had done—that was clear. The wildling was, too. Fer could fix the wildling with her herbs and spells, so maybe there was a way to fix the Lady's evil. Fer still wasn't sure what her place in this land was, but she knew her parents would have wanted her to help.

What she needed was to find out what the Lady had done to bring wrongness into the land. It had something to do with her mother, Fer felt almost certain, and with her father. With their deaths. Maybe the Lady had killed them for some reason.

But maybe it had nothing to do with them at all; maybe it was something done to this Leaf Woman they kept talking about.

Fer stood, her stomach jumping with nervousness. She

shoved Grand-Jane's note into her jeans pocket. "Don't worry, Grand-Jane," she said aloud. "I'll be careful."

Now she had the Lady's test to deal with. Whatever it was. Fer put on her warmest clothes and her patch-jacket and slung the quiver of arrows and her bow over her shoulder. Then she took the Lady's black feather out of the OWEN box and tucked it into the end of her braid. To leave it off would make the Lady suspicious.

She took a step toward the tent flap and then stopped and turned back. Opening the OWEN box again, she took out the letter her father had written to Grand-Jane and read it over. One part of it jumped out at her.

She is more beautiful and more wonderful than you could ever imagine, even without the glamorie . . .

The *glamorie*. Fer felt the power of the Lady's glamorie every time she looked at her. Like getting tangled up into a net. The glamorie's power was to compel obedience, Fer guessed. To make the one who wore it seem like something other than what she was. Fer hadn't seen what was hiding behind the Lady's glamorie, but she'd caught glimpses. And what she'd seen wasn't beautiful or powerful; it was a wildling thing, dark and terrifying.

Maybe . . . maybe the Lady wasn't really the Lady at

all. Maybe she was using the glamorie to hide what she really was.

Fer knew how to see through to the truth. Her hands shaking, she dug the seeing-stone out of the box and put it into her jacket pocket. She kept her hand there, gripping the stone for courage.

As she ducked out of her tent, she bumped into somebody dressed in a black coat. "Rook!" she exclaimed, stepping back. In the gray morning light he looked a little gray himself. But a lot better than yesterday. "Are you okay?"

He didn't answer her question. With narrowed eyes, he looked her up and down. "Ready?" he asked.

"I am," Fer said. "You're all better, aren't you? I healed your wolf bites?"

Rook shoved his hands into his coat pockets and glared down at the snowy ground. "You did, yes," he said. "Now I owe you a thrice-sworn oath for my life saved three times."

"I don't want a thrice-sworn oath from you, Rook," Fer said. "You know that."

"It doesn't matter whether you want it or not." One of the Lady's crow spies spiraled down and landed on Rook's shoulder. It squawked hoarsely into his ear. "All right, I'm coming," he muttered, then he roughly pushed the crow off; shedding feathers, it tumbled into the snow. Rook turned and headed down the path. "She sent me to fetch you," he said over his shoulder. "Come on. It's time."

Taking a deep breath, Fer gripped her bow and followed Rook along the snowy paths to the trampled area before the Lady's tent. A crowd was gathering, the Lady's people on one side, dressed in their ragged furs and their masks, their mounts held by badger-men among the shadowy pine trees beyond. Fer stopped and stood on her tiptoes, looking for Phouka. Not there yet. Her heart pounded with a mixture of excitement and fear. Whatever the Lady really was, she was going to find out today.

Other people besides the Lady's were waiting in the clearing. Little old men who looked like gray balls of yarn with red caps, and droopy old men with icicles in their ragged beards, and tall, slender young men with blond hair. All of them stood quietly, watching.

"Who are they?" Fer asked.

When Rook answered, his voice wasn't angry any more, just flat. "They are the Huldre's people. She is a Lady of this land."

Standing beside the doorway to the Lady's tent were two of the wolf-guards. Seeing Fer, they started across the clearing.

Rook stepped half in front of Fer, almost like he was

protecting her. "Back off," he said to the approaching guards.

The female wolf-guard grinned at him with yellow teeth. "Hey-ho, Pucky-toast!" She reached out and shoved Rook into a snowbank, then turned her grin on Fer. "Hey-ho, Fer-girlie."

"Hi," Fer said, trying to look past them to the Lady's tent.

"Need any butter or hot water or anything?" the female wolf-guard asked.

Fer shook her head. Her heart beat faster. She wasn't sure she could talk to the Lady without giving away her suspicions.

"All right. Good luck today." The female wolf-guard grabbed the other's arm—"Good luck!" he added—and dragged him back to their post by the tent flap.

"Thanks!" Fer called after them.

Rook stepped up beside her, scowling, brushing snow off his coat. "You're friends with the Lady's guards now?" he asked in a low voice.

"Not exactly friends," Fer said. She was about to explain about healing their wildling when she heard a snort. In the trees beyond the clearing, a badger-man held Phouka by his silver bridle. Fer smiled as Phouka jerked the bridle out of his groom's grip and, pushing two of the Lady's people out of the way with his nose, pranced across to Fer with his ears pricked.

"Hello, you bad horse," Fer said, reaching up to pat him on the velvety-soft nose. He would be her ally today. She needed one, at least. He whuffled into her hand, saying hello.

"Oh, sure," Rook said, glaring at Phouka. "Now *you're* friends with her too?"

"Yes, he is." Fer laid her cheek against Phouka's warm neck. The smell of horse was such a *good* smell. "Rook, you're my friend too."

"No, I am not," he answered.

"Yes, you are, whether you like it or not." Before he could argue with her, she pulled the seeing-stone out of her pocket. "Rook, my grandma told me that pucks have good vision. Can you see through the Lady's glamorie?"

He glared at her, staying stubbornly silent.

"She uses the glamorie to stop me from asking questions, doesn't she? And to make me see what she wants me to see. I'm wondering what I'll see if I look at her through this." She held up the seeing-stone.

Rook stepped closer, speaking in a fierce whisper. "Don't tell me anything, Fer. I'm bound. I'm not your friend. I can't help you."

Fer shoved the seeing-stone back into her pocket. "There's one more thing, Rook," she whispered back. She opened her mouth to tell him about the dying crown

176

she'd found in the Lady's tent, when the Lady herself emerged from her tent followed by a wizened old woman wearing a stained white dress with dusty fur at the hem.

"Ah, Gwynnefar," the Lady called, catching sight of Fer.

"Fer, be careful—" Rook said.

Over by the tent, the Lady beckoned.

"I will, Rook," Fer whispered back, and she left him and crossed the clearing to the Lady, who bent to kiss her on the forehead. Fer felt the Lady's chill magic settling over her; she blinked and shook her head, fighting to escape the net of her glamorie. She put her hand in her pocket, felt the smooth, cold seeing-stone under her fingers.

Straightening, the Lady saw Rook. "Join the others, Robin," she ordered, and Rook bowed and went to wait with the rest of the Lady's people.

Taking Fer by the shoulder, the Lady turned her to face the old woman. "This is the Huldre," the Lady said. "A Lady, as I am, who has begged for our help to bring the spring to her part of the land." She spoke to the Huldre. "This is Gwynnefar. Today she faces a test to see if she will take her place at my side as one of my most trusted people."

The Huldre, who had long, tangled white hair framing a rosy, wrinkled face, leaned closer, inspecting Fer.

"She will bring us the spring, then?" she asked.

The Lady gave a sharp nod. "The thing we discussed?"

The Huldre sighed. "All has been prepared, just as you ordered. You will pick up a trail in the forest to the east of here." She hobbled away to join her people on the other side of the clearing.

The Lady turned to speak to her own people. "We will begin soon. Gather your mounts and await me in the field."

As her people obeyed, Rook with them, the Lady turned and put her hands on Fer's shoulders. "You are ready?"

Fer gazed up at her. She shook her head to clear it. The Huldre had talked about a trail. And the Lady's people were all carrying bows and arrows, or sharp spears, she'd noticed. "Is this test a hunt?"

The Lady shook her head, as if in sadness. "Again you demand answers from me. I am not your enemy, Gwynnefar. I brought you here to this land because I need your help. My people tell me you like to help, is that right?"

Fer blinked. "Yes, I do," she answered.

"Good," the Lady said. "You are a warrior, as your mother was, and you alone can complete the ritual that will bring the spring, both here and on the other side of the Way."

Fer frowned, her suspicion growing. "I thought *you*

brought the spring." That's what Rook had told her, anyway.

The Lady's face stayed still and cold. "My power is . . . not what it once was. You can help renew my power. Then all will be as it should. You have learned quickly; you can ride and shoot. You were born to take your mother's place by my side, Gwynnefar."

Fer wrenched her eyes away from the Lady's intent face. It wasn't time to use the seeing-stone—not yet. First she had to be strong; she had to *think*. She held up her bow. "Your test is a hunt. I'm not killing anything, even if my mother *was* a huntress."

The Lady's hands gripped harder. "The test is a ritual, as I told you," she said sharply. "You will do as you must when the moment comes. Your mother would have done the same for me. Now, we must hurry." She released Fer's shoulders and stepped back.

A badger-man came up, leading the Lady's white horse. The Lady swung gracefully onto its back, then took the bow and quiver of arrows the badger-man handed up to her.

More weapons. Fer shivered, partly with cold, partly with nervousness.

The Lady took a deep breath. "I know you suspect that something is wrong here. You are correct. We both want the same thing, Gwynnefar. We want to right what is wrong." She looked away, then fixed Fer again with her glimmering eyes, turning the full force of her glamorie onto Fer. "It is your duty to help me."

Fer closed her eyes against the spell. The Lady was dangerous. But she was convincing, too. She and Fer did want the same thing—they both wanted to bring the spring, here and at home, to fix the wrongness in the land that Fer could feel with every breath, with every step she took on the frozen ground. If passing the test and completing the spring ritual would fix the wrongness, then she would do it. Fer still didn't trust the Lady, but she would go along with her—for now. Opening her eyes, Fer nodded. "All right," she agreed. "I will help you."

seventeen

Just as the Huldre had said, they picked up a trail in the forest to the east of the field, not far from where Fer and the Lady had ridden their horses the day before. The sun came up, and the sky turned brilliant blue. The air was bitterly cold as they set off.

The Lady led the way, her crows flying overhead. Fer rode at her right, finding her balance on Phouka's back, gripping his mane and her bow, which was strung and ready, feeling the weight of the quiver full of arrows over her shoulder. Behind them rode the rest of the Lady's people, mounted on tall horses and shaggy ponies, and on the backs of deer and curly-horned goats. The three wolf-guards were among them. Rook was there too, riding behind a badger-man on a chestnut horse.

The Lady had Fer dismount to check the trail. They crouched in the snow, looking at it. To Fer the trail looked not like footprints, but like scufflings in the snow. They didn't look like the hoofprints of a deer, anyway.

The Lady pointed with a gloved hand. "You see here, Gwynnefar? The distinct edges? The distance between the prints?"

Fer nodded.

"This indicates that the trail is still fresh." The Lady stood and brushed the snow from her knees. Her people and their mounts waited like shadows among the trees; her crows wheeled overhead, cawing.

"What are we chasing?" Fer asked, but the Lady was already turning away, mounting her horse.

Fer belly-flopped onto Phouka's back and found her place riding beside the Lady. They rode without speaking, and the forest around them was silent except for a wind that hissed in the tops of the pine trees. After a while, the trail led them out of the dark forest and through a valley to a wide plain bare of trees. On the plain the wind grew even more bitter, sweeping up plumes of snow before it. In the distance, Fer saw low hills building to rocky foothills and, beyond them, mountain peaks. Seeing them, her heart lifted. She'd sensed them the day before, but she'd never actually seen real, live mountains.

They rode on. Fer's fingers were stiff with cold. She

slung the bow over her shoulder with the quiver and alternated holding Phouka's mane with one hand while putting the other hand in her patch-jacket pocket to warm it up. Phouka himself snorted out clouds of steam and kept steady pace with the Lady and her horse, while the rest of the Mór's people strung out behind them as their mounts tired. Fer felt the Lady's eyes on her, watching, waiting, Fer guessed, to see what she would do.

At midday they entered another forest, and the Lady got down to check the trail. "We have time for a short rest," she said.

Fer slid down from Phouka's back and patted his neck. Her legs felt a little stiff, but not too bad.

"You are doing well on the test, Gwynnefar," the Lady said. "It is good to have you riding at my side, just as your mother once did."

Fer knew she was doing well. Still, she felt like a rope inside her chest was twisting tighter and tighter as the hunt continued.

The wolf-guards caught up and dismounted and handed around food from their saddlebags: bread and cheese, which Fer ate, and strips of dried meat, which she didn't. The rest of the Lady's people straggled in too. The badger-man and Rook came in at last on their chestnut horse. Rook kept his head down, not meeting Fer's eyes when she looked over at him.

After a few minutes, the Lady gave the order to mount up again, and they were off, trotting through the bare-branched trees. They rode for the rest of the afternoon over the forested hills, following the muffled trail.

As the shadows grew longer, Fer caught a glimpse ahead of them of something moving among the trees, a flash of gray against the white snow.

"There!" The Lady pointed, then shouted something over her shoulder at the rest of her people.

Fer gripped Phouka's mane and held on as he leaped into a fast gallop. Beside her, the Lady crouched over her horse's shoulders, urging it to go faster. The sudden wind blew tears from Fer's eyes. She blinked them away and focused ahead, watching between Phouka's ears for another glimpse of the thing she'd seen before. From behind came the high, thin call of the hunting horn.

The thing had dodged off to the side. "That way!" the Lady shouted, pointing. Fer gave Phouka a nudge with her knee, following. The horse leaned as he turned, and she leaned with him. They zigzagged among the black trees, right behind the Lady, silent in the snow except for the horses' snorting breath. The other riders and their mounts fell away as they raced faster through the trees. Another glimpse of gray, of something running, sending up clouds of snow.

The setting sun crouched at the top of the hill, shedding fiery light over the forest. At the base of the hill was a clearing bound on one side by a steep cliff of rock. Phouka burst from the trees at the edge of the clearing, and Fer saw the thing they chased scramble up the cliff face to a narrow shelf about six feet off the ground.

In the shadows, against the gray cliff, the thing was hard to make out. Was it an animal? Phouka halted, breathing hard.

The Lady pulled up beside her. "Ah," she panted. "It is at bay."

"What *is* it?" Fer asked, squinting to see better.

"Our prey," the Lady said sharply. She reached back into her quiver and drew out an arrow, which she held out to Fer. "Here. Use this."

Fer took the arrow. It was fletched with black crow feathers, the shaft smooth and black, the point made of blackened, barbed steel. Fer gripped the arrow and looked up at the Lady. Her heart started pounding. "But I told you. I can't kill anything."

"This is the ritual," the Lady said. "You must complete it to bring spring to this land." Behind the Lady, the other hunters, riding their exhausted mounts, entered the clearing and halted, waiting silently, watching. Rook was among them.

The prey. It cowered against the cliff face above her, panting, every breath sending out gusts of steam in the icy air. Blood foamed at its mouth, as if it had run until its lungs were bursting. Its skin was lumpy and gray, and

185

it had long arms wrapped around its barrel-shaped middle. Its legs were as thick as tree trunks and its head was like a boulder with a rough, heavy-browed face carved out of it. A troll.

Holding her bow, Fer climbed down from Phouka's back.

From behind her, the Lady spoke. "Kill it, Gwynnefar. It is just a thing, a base creature, a blood sacrifice. If you truly wish to serve me as your mother did, to help drive winter from the land, you must complete the ritual."

Fer felt the full power of the Lady's glamorie fall over her like a spiked silver net. With chilled fingers, she fitted the black arrow onto the string and raised the bow, then drew back the string and sighted down the arrow at the gray troll on the cliff. She felt the shot settle within her. She would release the bowstring and the arrow would fly straight and true to its target.

The troll turned to the wall and ducked to hide its face in its hands.

Fer closed her eyes and saw again the stag in the moonlit clearing, its frightened eyes, the hunt that had ended with blood and death at the hands of the Lady.

"Spill its blood," the Lady said, her voice pulsing with command. "You *must*."

Fer lowered the bow and turned to face the Lady. Raising her hand, Fer felt a sudden surge of power, and she brushed the glamorie away, just like brushing a sticky cobweb out of her eyes. "I won't do it."

The Lady stared down from her horse's back, her face white and set. "You would fail me, and all my people, and this land because you are afraid to shed blood?"

"It's not because I'm afraid," Fer said, shivering. She tore her gaze away from the Lady's beautiful face and looked down at the black arrow, smooth and sharp and deadly. Her mother, Laurelin, had never done anything like this. If the Lady had to kill something to bring the spring, then her magic was broken. It was *wrong*. Spring was about life and green buds and birdsong, not about hunting a living creature to a bloody death.

Slinging her bow over her shoulder, Fer gripped the arrow at both ends, broke it across her knee, and dropped it in the snow. Behind her she heard a scuffling sound, and turned to see the troll jump down from the cliff and shamble out of the clearing, dragging its knuckles through the snow. The Lady's people stirred, as if they wanted to go after the troll, but the Lady raised her hand, holding them.

Then, with a jolt, Fer remembered the seeing-stone in her patch-jacket pocket. It was time to use it, to see what the Lady truly was. With shaking hands she pulled out the stone and held it up to her eye. As she looked, the Lady flinched away and her horse reared, and Fer glimpsed only a swirl of ragged feathers and the Lady's sharp, darting eyes, not beautiful at all, not a Lady, but something terribly wrong.

Fer stumbled back. She felt a nudge against her shoulder, then warm breath on her neck. Phouka, like a sturdy wall behind her. She shot a glance at the Lady's people. In the shadows at the edge of the clearing, dressed in furs and rags, with their fanged and horned masks, they looked like wild creatures. Through her connection to them, she felt how their strength was fading. Soon they'd be nothing more than wild animals, completely lost to themselves.

Rook stood among them. She caught his eye.

He gave a slight nod toward the edge of the clearing, then mouthed an urgent word. *Run.*

"The hunt must go on," the Lady said. She sat like a pale, stone statue on her horse's back. She was still beautiful, but the glamorie no longer had any power over Fer. Deliberately the Lady reached over her shoulder and drew an arrow from her quiver. A black arrow, just like the one she'd given Fer to use on the troll. She fit the arrow onto her bowstring and raised the bow. "Blood must be spilled," the Lady said coldly. "If you will not serve me, Gwynnefar, then you must become prey."

"No!" Fer shouted. The Lady drew the bow. Trembling, Fer backed into Phouka, then ducked right under his belly. Reaching up, she grabbed his mane and flung herself onto his back. "Go, Phouka!" she shouted, and before she could sit straight he was off and running, jolting into a gallop as she dragged her leg over his back. Looking over her shoulder, Fer saw an arrow speeding toward her. She flinched, hunching into her patch-jacket, hoping it would protect her, and the arrow bent away and buried itself in a tree. The Lady drew another black arrow from the quiver, and then Phouka dodged around a tree and the clearing was gone. The gray twilight closed in around them.

"Take me to the Way, Phouka," Fer gasped. "Take me home."

eighteen

"After her!" the Mór shrieked. She wheeled her horse, which took two stumbling steps and then stopped, its head hanging. The rest of her people and their mounts stirred, but they, too, were exhausted from the day's hunt. Even her crows, hunched in the trees, looked bedraggled and tired.

Rook edged behind the brown horse he'd been riding. A crow perched in a nearby tree cackled, drawing the Mór's eye, and she saw him.

She jammed her arrow back into the quiver. Rook saw that her face was pinched and white, her hands gripping her horse's mane like shriveled claws. "Robin," she croaked. "Come here."

His thrice-sworn oath felt like a weighted chain

around his neck. He stepped away from the rest of the Mór's people.

"You, at least, are fresh," the Mór muttered. She dug into her trouser pocket, pulled something out, and tossed it to him.

His shifter-bone.

"Shift," she ordered. "Go after the traitorous girl and your twice-traitorous puck-brother, and hold them until I arrive."

Rook clenched his fists, feeling the shifter-bone bite into his palm. He shook his head. "Just let them go."

The Mór leaned forward. "You are bound, Puck," she snarled. "Catch them and hold them!"

His oath tightened around him; he had to obey. He whirled away from the Mór and took two running steps, then popped the bone into his mouth. As it settled under his tongue he felt the wonderful, free feeling of the shift, falling forward and catching himself on four hoofs, his mane and tail unfurling in the wind.

Leaving the Mór and her people behind, he galloped through the trees, following the trail Phouka had left in the snow. As the night closed in around him, the trail went up a wooded hill and disappeared and he followed it, leaping up into the sky in great bounds, the stars shooting past him, the air bitterly cold.

Ahead, he knew Fer was clinging to Phouka's mane,

cold and frightened, but, if he knew Fer, she was feeling brave, too, and ready to fight. She was trying to get to the Way. He had his orders, and he was bound. He would catch her if he could.

On he raced through the night, the wind rushing past him. His four hooves pounded the sky as he flew through clouds, darkness yawning below him. After a long time, the sky around him turned gray. His legs grew tired; his stride faltered and his breath came in snorting gusts.

A sudden jolt and he was galloping through a blurred gray and brown forest. The world spun around him and he fell into a trot on the path leading to the Way. Gnarled branches arched overhead. Fog hovered knee deep over the ground like the ghost of snow.

Ahead he glimpsed Phouka, Fer crouched and clinging to his back. Putting on a last burst of speed he reached the clearing. The Way waited for Fer, shimmering pearly white in the foggy morning light.

Rook stumbled to a halt.

Fer slid off of Phouka's back and leaned against his shoulder, looking cold and stiff. Phouka stood with his head hanging down, his ears drooping.

Rook found the shifter-bone under his tongue and spat it out, then felt the blurring dizziness of the change and caught the bone in his hand, standing on two legs. He shoved the shifter-bone into his coat pocket.

"Rook?" Fer gasped. Her wild, honey-colored hair

was tangled, her eyes bright, her cheeks chapped pink from the cold. Beside her, Phouka gave a low whinny. She patted his neck. "Is she coming?"

Fer looked as weary as he felt. He took a shaky step toward her. "She is, yes. I'm under orders to hold you and Phouka until she arrives."

Her face went pale and her eyes widened.

"I told you I wasn't your friend," he said roughly. But no, she hadn't listened. She didn't understand how strongly an oath sworn three times bound one of his kind. He had no choice.

Fer glanced over her shoulder at the Way.

Rook edged closer, ready to spring after her if she tried to use the Way to escape.

But she didn't move. "Rook," she said. "I snuck into the Lady's tent and looked in the box where she keeps her stuff. I found a crown made of leaves."

He nodded. "The Lady's crown." She was stalling, trying to distract him, but it wouldn't work. He edged closer. Beside her, Phouka snorted a warning.

"Rook," Fer said urgently. "The crown was dying. The Lady has done something evil, and it's hurting her people and the land."

Rook nodded stiffly. Yes, he knew. He couldn't tell her, but he knew.

Fer went on, her gray eyes intent. "Rook, things are wrong here. The wildling, the Leaf Woman missing, this terrible hunt ritual the Lady, or whatever she is, uses to bring the springtime. You know it's wrong. She was ready to kill me. I think you know what she did before. You have to tell me!"

Rook shook his head, feeling dizzy and sick. "I'm under orders, Fer," he said wearily. "There's nothing to be done." He'd been stupid to think maybe this girl from the other side of the Way could help. She'd proven to be surprisingly powerful, but he should have realized that it had been too late from the start. The blood had been spilled. The land had fallen under a shadow, and not even Fer could lift it. All was lost.

From not too far down the path, Rook heard a howl. The wolf-guards would be here in a moment. All was lost, and Fer was to become the next sacrifice.

Fer stepped toward him. "Then come through the Way with me, Rook. You'll be free of her there."

"Fer, I am bound," he warned. She should have flinched away, but she stood steady, trusting, holding out her hand.

He reached for it. Instead of taking her hand, he grabbed her wrist.

Fer pulled away, but he gripped her tightly.

From behind him, out of the fog, came three gray shapes. The wolves loped into the clearing with their tongues lolling, fog swirling around them. Rook saw Fer grope in her patch-jacket pocket. Feeling for her bag of spelled herbs, he knew, so she could force the wolves to stay away. But no, she'd used the herbs to heal him. She had no protection.

The wolves paced closer.

Fer glanced over her shoulder at the Way. The surface of the pool was as clear as glass, the fog drifting away. "Let me go," she panted.

He wanted to, more than anything. "No," he growled.

"Rook, you know the Lady is evil. She can't be the real Lady! Doesn't that mean you're free of her?"

No matter what the Mór had done, he was still bound by his oaths to her. He shook his head.

She pulled away and kicked him in the shin, but he tightened his grip and dragged her farther from the pool. In the distance, he heard galloping hoofbeats. The Mór, coming with her bow and her black arrows.

From behind Fer, Phouka gave a high whinny; then he stepped past her and nudged Rook's shoulder with his nose.

"Get off," he snarled, shrugging the horse away.

With an angry snort, Phouka reared back and kicked with his front hooves, knocking Rook's grip loose. Fer jerked her arm out of his hands and stumbled away. Rook reached after her, but Phouka lunged forward and shoved him to the ground, then dropped his heavy hoof on his shoulder, holding him down.

Growling, one of the wolves circled Phouka, coming for Fer. The horse kicked out with a back hoof, and the wolf went flying with a yelp.

The other two wolves snarled and leaped toward Fer. *Look out!* Rook wanted to shout.

A wolf tore at Fer's jacket, its teeth slashing into her arm. Blood spattered.

Fer whirled, took two steps, and jumped into the Way.

nineteen

Fer landed in rushing, dark water. She caught a wet gasp and was swept along. The world was loud with the sound of racing water and wind and thunder. Her back bumped against something and she flung out an arm and grabbed for it. Slick, wet branches—a bush. She held on against the water's strong pull and slowly dragged herself out, her patch-jacket sodden, the bow and quiver of arrows heavy on her back, her hair dripping.

A fierce flash of lighting rent the sky, followed a second later by a roar of thunder. Greenish-black clouds were piled in a dark mass overhead; the wind shrieked; rain pelted down. Coughing, Fer blinked the rain out of her eyes and dragged herself farther from the rushing water. Her arm burned where the wolf's teeth had slashed her. She climbed shakily to her feet, clinging to a wet tree trunk to steady herself, and tried to get her bearings.

The Way was pounded by the rain. The stream leading into it was now a dark, swift, rushing river. She waited a moment to see if the wolves, or Rook, or the Lady would follow her through. But nothing came through the flooded Way.

Safe. The Lady had tried to kill her, and Rook had betrayed her, and she'd left poor Phouka behind, but she was safe. For now. With a sob, she stumbled back, and brambles clung to her patch-jacket. Tearing herself free, her feet slipping on mud and wet leaves, she ran along the edge of the swollen stream until she hit the path, then followed that out to the culvert and the straight gravel road.

Thunder bellowed again, and Fer flinched. Over her head the clouds boiled, and bitter hail pelted down. The fields, as far as she could see in the murky light, were flooded. In the distance she saw the Carsons' farm like an inkblot on the watery horizon. But it didn't look right—the dark shape of the barn was missing. Lashed by wind and hail, Fer ran along the edge of the muddy road, cutting across a soggy field that left her splattered with mud up to her knees, then to the long, puddled driveway to her house. Two of the oak trees were down across the driveway, their leafless branches spread like tangled nets to catch her. Dodging them, half panting, half crying, she ran around to the back door, up the steps, and burst into the kitchen.

Grand-Jane appeared at the door to the stillroom. Seeing Fer, her eyes widened. Two steps and Fer was across the kitchen and in her grandma's arms, and Grand-Jane was hugging her tightly, saying, "Oh, my dear girl."

Fer clung to her for a long time, until she caught her breath and felt Grand-Jane's hand stroking her wet hair. She sighed and stepped back.

Grand-Jane rested her hands on Fer's shoulders. "You're all right?"

Fer nodded and scrubbed the tears out of her eyes. "My arm."

Grand-Jane gently took the bow and quiver of arrows from her, then guided her to a chair and sat her down. After helping Fer take off the patch-jacket, she went to the stillroom to mix up a healing poultice. She said a few words, but Fer heard a whirling in her ears, the sound of the wind when she and Phouka had ridden through the sky all night long, and then everything went black.

She woke up in the dark, snug and dry and safe in her own bed under her patchwork quilt. Rain pounded on the roof over her head and wind howled around the house, shaking the windows in their frames. Slowly she sat up, feeling the ache in her bones of the hunt and the long ride after it all. She switched on the lamp beside her bed. Around one forearm, where the wolf had bitten her, was a clean white bandage. Under it, the wound ached. Around her right wrist was a nasty blue-black bruise from where Rook had gripped her.

Stupid, stubborn Rook. She took a shaky breath. Or, maybe, honorable Rook, holding to his oath. She wasn't sure which.

Getting out of bed, the wooden floor cold on her bare feet, she put on her bathrobe over her nightgown and went to the window. Rain streamed down the glass; beyond that was only darkness.

Grand-Jane had said in her letter that things were bad. Fer hadn't realized how bad. All because of the open Way and the wrongness on the other side of it. She shivered.

Then her stomach growled. When had she last eaten? Breakfast before the hunt. It felt like days ago. Nine fifteen, the clock on her bedside table said. Not too late for dinner.

She padded down to the warm, red-and-yellow kitchen, where Grand-Jane was sitting at the table stitching up the rips and the wolf bite in Fer's patch-jacket, her sewing basket on the floor beside her chair. The bow and quiver were leaning against the wall by the door.

Fer paused in the doorway. "Hi," she said. Her voice sounded hoarse.

Grand-Jane looked at her over the rims of her reading

glasses. "You're up." She set down her needle and thread and Fer's jacket and got to her feet. "The kettle's on the boil. Come and sit down and have tea, and then I'll make you some eggs and toast."

Fer hobbled to a chair and creaked down into it. "How long was I gone?" she asked.

"Just over six weeks," Grand-Jane answered, setting a steaming mug before her on the table. "I was getting worried."

Fer could tell from the way Grand-Jane said it that what she felt went far beyond worry. "It didn't seem like that long," she said.

"Time passes differently there," Grand-Jane said. "But you held to your promise. You came back."

Fer remembered something that had bothered her on her way home. "Did something happen to the Carsons' farm?"

Grand-Jane nodded. "A tornado destroyed their barn. The storms have been very bad."

Yes, Fer could see that. Grand-Jane bent to kiss Fer on the temple. "What's this?" She pulled something from Fer's tangled hair.

The Lady's black feather. Fer took it from her grand-mother.

Grand-Jane sat down at the table, picking up her mending again. "Tell me what happened."

There was so much to tell. With shaking fingers, Fer

smoothed the ruffled feather and set it on the table. She sniffed the steam rising from her mug. Nettle tea, for healing and protection. She took a sip. Honey in it too, made from nectar the bees had gathered from the fields of lavender. Leave it to Grand-Jane to know exactly what she needed. "Something is wrong there," Fer said. Her voice shook a little. "That's why things are so bad here."

Grand-Jane nodded.

She told her grandma about the wildlings and how she'd cured them with spells and herbs, and after Grand-Jane had asked questions about which herbs and which spells, and approved what she'd done, Fer told about the bloody hunt that was supposed to bring the spring, and her guess that something the Lady had done was behind everything that was wrong.

"And Owen?" Grand-Jane asked. "What did you find out about him?"

Fer shook her head. "I think Rook knows what happened, but he couldn't tell me anything."

"Rook?" Grand-Jane asked, and with scissors from her sewing basket snipped off a thread.

"The puck," Fer explained. "He's—" She paused and took a shaky breath. "I think he's my friend. He owes a thrice-sworn oath to the Lady."

Grand-Jane frowned. "Thrice-sworn?" She shook her head. "I don't think he was your friend, Jennifer."

Fer cupped her hands around the mug of tea. Rook. She'd left him next to the moon-pool, pinned to the ground under Phouka's hoof. What had happened after that?

She had one more question. "Grand-Jane, did you ever meet my mother?"

Her grandma bowed her head over her sewing, but she didn't take a stitch. "I saw her once. I followed Owen to the crossing place. He was going to meet her, and I tried to stop him, because I knew he was putting himself in danger. He was more a boy than a man then. We argued." She sighed. "Then I saw her, and I knew that I'd lost him forever."

"What was she like?" Fer asked. She thought she knew, from her dream, but she had to be sure.

"Beautiful, of course," Grand-Jane answered. She took a stitch. "But she wasn't what I expected."

"What was she?"

"I saw her take off the glamour, the magic that made her beautiful, and I saw that she was just a girl, not so much older than you are."

"She really did love my father," Fer said. Not a question. She knew it to be true.

"I think she did," Grand-Jane answered softly.

Fer nodded. *That* was the story she'd been trying to find. But she still didn't know its ending.

After a silent while, Grand-Jane folded Fer's mended jacket. "Well, my girl," she said, getting to her feet. "There is nothing more you can do. We will go first thing tomorrow and you will close the Way, and that will be an end to it. You'd better drink up your tea and have some dinner, and then it's back to bed with you."

In the morning, Fer found herself stiff and sore and standing with Grand-Jane on the gravel road by the culvert, the roar and rush of the stream loud in her ears. The storm had stopped, but the sky was gray and the wind was cold, and a slick of ice covered the flooded fields. In a puddle near her feet she saw three sodden balls of matted fur, half-covered with muddy water. When she squatted down to see what they were, she found three baby raccoons, drowned and dead. Everything was dying—the land, the animals, everything. Shivering, Fer stood and pulled the sleeves of her patch-jacket over her hands. While she'd been gone, the school year had ended. It was supposed to be summertime.

On the walk over, her grandma had told Fer more about the terrible weather. With all the rain, the basement of the public library had flooded and the entire collection of books was lost to mold. Farmers had tried planting their corn and soybeans, and the seeds had rotted in the ground. Grand-Jane had turned over the mud in her herb gardens, but her seeds and cuttings didn't come up either. Outside in the trees, birds' eggs were rotting in their nests.

And Grand-Jane's bees were still asleep in their hives. They would die soon without sun and fields of flowers.

All of those bad things were happening because the Way was open.

"Go quickly," Grand-Jane said. "And be careful. Close the Way and come back here. I'll wait for you."

Fer nodded to Grand-Jane and slipped down the bank. The rushing stream had overflowed its banks and ran right next to the path, which was muddy and slick. Fer went along the path, clinging to branches on the other side when she slipped. After pushing through a clump of bushes, she came to the pool, which was brown and swollen with rainwater and had flooded its mossy banks, but it wasn't the roiling torrent it'd been the night before, when she'd come through.

When she'd opened the Way, she'd touched the surface of the water and felt a tingle, almost like a shock, as it had opened. Crouching, she held her fingers just over the water. Wavelets rippled across the pool, which reflected the gloomy gray sky overhead. Fer felt the same tingling tightness in her chest that she had before, a power inside her. With a touch she could make it go away, and the Way would be closed and all its wrongness would stop troubling her world. She brought her fingers closer to the rippling surface of the water.

Time was passing in the other place. What was happening there? The more Fer thought about it, the more certain she was that Rook had gotten into trouble. To the Lady, arriving at the moon-pool just as Fer had jumped, it would look like Rook had let Fer get away. And poor, brave Phouka. Just thinking about him made Fer shiver. The Lady would use a whip on a horse she thought was disobedient.

If Fer closed the Way, it would mean Rook, and Phouka, and Twig and Burr, and the wolf-guards—all of them would be lost to the Lady and the evil she'd loosed upon her land. Nothing would have been set right.

She took a deep breath, then stood up and shoved her chilled hands into her patch-jacket pockets. Then she looked around at the bedraggled clearing, the flooded pool. As long as the Way was open, the wrongness would keep spilling over into her world.

"I have to go back," she whispered to herself. Then she nodded, feeling more certain. She had to leave the Way open, to be sure she could get back there and right the wrongness, and she had to do it fast, before things here got any worse.

But she had some things to figure out first.

❋ ❋ ❋

When they got home, Grand-Jane went to sit at the kitchen table with the account books for her herb and honey business spread out on the table. As Fer came in with an armful of books, she set down her pencil. "What are you up to, my girl?"

Fer set the books down on the table with a thump. "Studying." She lifted Hildegard's *Causae et Curae* and showed her grandma the cover.

Grand-Jane looked at Fer over the rims of her reading glasses. "All right," she said mildly. "Would you like tea?"

Fer shook her head, set the herbology book aside, and opened the leather-bound journal she'd found beside it on the bookshelf. The handwriting was old-fashioned, the ink fading, the pages yellowed. It contained notes on herbs and spells, but also on the *others*, as the writer called them. Some of the things Fer knew already, things her grandma had told her about oaths and the power of asking questions three times, and she found a few sentences about how turning your clothes inside out made a person invisible to the others. That explained why her patch-jacket's brown lining had hidden her from the Lady's people on the night she'd snuck into the Lady's tent. But that wasn't what she was looking for. She felt the Way tugging at her, reminding her to hurry. Grand-Jane placed a hot cup of tea at her elbow, but it grew cool as she read on.

At last she came to a section labeled "Rites and Rituals." There she found what she'd been looking for. She read the spidery script once, then again to be sure she understood it.

The Green Man: The year for the others begins with spring, and the wheel of the seasons is set turning by the Green Man, who is sometimes a Woman. It is the Green Man's power and purpose to bring the spring to all the Lands through a life-giving ritual that is followed by celebrations as the darkness of winter is banished and Green returns to the Land.

Fer nodded. *Life-giving ritual*. Not bloodshed and death.

She knew what she had to do.

twenty

Fer stood ankle-deep in water at the edge of the flooded moon-pool, her heart pounding with excitement and fright. Her arm ached a little where the wolf had bitten her. The day was gray and gloomy, the sun hidden behind a blanket of clouds. Fer could feel the wrongness in the air, spilling through the open Way.

Over one shoulder she had her quiver full of arrows and her bow. On the other she had a heavy backpack. It was stuffed with bags of herbs and vials of tincture she'd stolen from the stillroom, and also with extra socks, a blanket, matches and a candle, a canteen full of water, and food. In each of her patch-jacket pockets, she had a cloth bag of spelled herbs for protection. She felt as if needles were prickling all over her skin. At every ripple of water that passed over the moon-pool she felt another prickle.

Early in the morning, before Grand-Jane was awake, she'd gotten the backpack and the bow and quiver of arrows ready, and she'd snuck out. She hadn't left a note—Grand-Jane would guess where she'd gone. Then she'd headed down the roads to the culvert and along the ravine, which was awash in rushing water. Fer had been forced to pick her way along the edges of the flooded stream, and still her sneakers were soaking, and her jeans were wet up to her knees.

At the edge of the clearing around the moon-pool, the leafless branches rustled in the breeze. Fer stared down at the surface of the water. She was doing the right thing, running away. She *was*. Wavelets rippled across the pool, and then the water stilled. Fer felt her breath come short and her heart beat faster.

Time to go. She jumped.

Fer landed on mossy ground beside the pool.

It looked exactly the same, though not as wet. Moss, bare branches, bushes covered with rustling brown leaves. The Lady had used her hunt of the stag to bring the spring here before, but the power was fading because it was a false ritual done by a false Lady. The spring was slipping back into winter.

Hearing a low growl, Fer sat up. Across the pool from her, standing stiff-legged, was a shaggy black dog with yellow eyes. One of his ears stuck up; the other was lopped over.

Fer scrambled to her feet. "Rook?" she asked.

He lowered his head and growled again.

It sounded like Rook, anyway. Fer edged around the pool, ready to run if she had to. "Did the Lady leave you here to catch me if I came back?"

The dog just looked at her.

Fer stepped closer. His yellow eyes looked like they had little flames dancing in them. She blinked and for a second she saw Rook as he would look to anybody else, a huge, fierce dog with sharp teeth, fiery eyes, and shaggy fur. But she wasn't afraid of him. "Well, change back into a boy, Rook, so you can talk to me."

He didn't move.

Oh. Fer's heart gave a little jolt. "You're stuck as a dog, aren't you," she said. "Just like Phouka is stuck as a horse?"

After a silent moment, the dog tipped his head down. Like a nod.

"She did this? As punishment?" Fer asked.

Again the tip of the head.

"For breaking your thrice-sworn oath?"

The dog bared his teeth and growled.

Fer almost felt like laughing. Rook was a dog, but he was still Rook. "Okay, I know you didn't break your oath," she said. Still, it wasn't fair. The Lady had to be punishing Rook for letting Fer escape through the Way, even though he'd tried to stop her. "Do you still serve her?"

The dog gave her a long, yellow-eyed stare.

He did, then. But somehow he'd gotten away from the Lady, and maybe he would help. Fer continued around the edge of the pool. As she got close to him, he backed up a few steps, his fur bristling. She crouched down in front of him and reached out her hand. "It's okay, Rook," she whispered.

He stayed back, watching her warily.

"Is Phouka all right?" Fer asked.

No head tip, just the yellow-eyed stare. He wasn't, then. Fer gulped down a knot of worry and got to her feet.

The dog cocked his head, listening to something Fer couldn't hear. Suddenly he lunged forward and, before Fer could dodge out of the way, seized the hem of her jacket in his teeth and started pulling her toward the forest.

In the distance, Fer heard the howl of a wolf. She whirled, jerking her jacket out of Rook's jaws, and looked down the path leading into the forest.

Rook gave a low bark and ran to the edge of the forest

where another, narrower path led away; he paused and looked back at her, waiting.

"Let's go." Fer followed Rook out of the moon-pool clearing and into the end-of-winter forest. Rook broke into a loping run. Her backpack, bow, and quiver heavy on her shoulders, Fer ran to keep up. "Slow . . . down, Rook," Fer gasped. "You have four legs and I only have two."

They ran for what seemed to Fer like hours, until the straps of the heavy backpack were digging into her shoulders, her breath came in gasps, and her legs felt like sacks filled with wet cement. The trail grew narrower and the light grew dim as the sun set. A twig slashed Fer across the face. A clump of brambles spilled out onto the path and tripped her feet. She stumbled to a stop and bent over, panting.

Rook loped back. In the growing darkness he seemed to float over the ground like a shadow.

Fer straightened and tried to still her breath so she could listen for the wolf-guards. "I don't . . . hear them," she said. "Let's camp here."

As an answer, the dog padded off the path to a murky clearing in the woods where a dead tree had fallen. Fer followed. Panting, Rook flopped down on the wiry brown grass, and Fer slung her backpack, bow, and quiver on the ground. Then she crouched down so she'd be closer to eye level with Rook. "I guess we can't risk having a fire if those wolves are hunting for us." She dug in her backpack until she found matches and the wax candle she'd stolen from the stillroom. After lighting the candle, which Grand-Jane had scented with rowan and rosemary for protection, she brought out the packets of food. "Hungry?" she asked.

Rook jumped to his paws and leaped into the circle of wavering candlelight.

Fer tossed him a piece of cheese, and he snapped it down before it even hit the ground. She laid out the rest of the dinner on her blanket. Rook took exactly half, leaving the rest for Fer to eat more slowly.

When she'd finished, she wrapped herself in her blanket and blew out the candle. The clearing was completely dark. Fer heard the rustle of a breeze in the naked tree branches overhead. An arm's length away, Rook lay down, his eyes gleaming in the darkness. She'd be safe, she knew, as long as he was watching.

twenty-one

Rook kept watch all night. His nose sifted information from the breeze. A deer had passed through the clearing a few hours ago. Mice were building a nest in a rotting log. Wolves were . . . He stood and paced to the path, sniffing. Wolves were not nearby.

He padded back to the clearing to check on Fer, who lay sound asleep wrapped in her blanket. She smelled like the lavender and magical herbs in her jacket pockets, and her honey-colored hair smelled like she'd washed it with some other herbs.

The sky overhead was tinged with gray, very early morning. Dew covered the wiry grass. A tendril of scent drifted under his nose. Following it, he came to a den made of dried grass, inhabited by two sleeping rabbits.

Breakfast! He killed them both with a quick snap of his jaws, then devoured one. His stomach had been hollow for such a long time, since the Mór had forced him to shift to dog form, and with the dinner Fer had given him the night before and now this good rabbit breakfast, he felt better. Not quite so snappish.

Leaving the fur and bones of his breakfast, he took the limp body of the other rabbit in his jaws and loped back to the clearing.

Fer was just waking, sitting up with her damp blanket wrapped around her and her hair sticking up around her head. "Hi, Rook," she said. Her voice sounded rusty with sleep.

He bounded up and lay the rabbit before her.

She blinked, then shifted away. "What is that? A dead squirrel?"

No, it's a rabbit, stupid. He pushed it closer to her with his nose.

"Oh, it's supposed to be breakfast?"

It is. Eat it. We have to get moving.

She climbed to her feet, shedding the wet blanket. "Um, Rook? I don't eat meat. Ever."

She didn't eat meat? He'd never heard of anything so stupid. Still, it meant more breakfast for him. He leaped on the rabbit and tore into it.

"Ugh," Fer said, and turned away while she finished eating her own breakfast.

Once they'd finished, she packed her things again and sat on the log. "Rook, do you know why I came back?"

He knew. When she'd first come through the Way, she'd just been a girl, but now she was bound to the land and its people. She'd come back to save them, even though her cause was hopeless. The land was doomed, and its people would turn wildling one by one as the Mór grew more depraved. Fer would never defeat the Mór. Still, he would help her until the Mór caught him and punished him for pushing at the boundaries of his oath. This time she'd kill him for it, he knew. But that didn't matter anymore.

Fer went on. "I read in a book about the ritual, the bringing of spring. It's the Leaf Woman I saw, and that I kept hearing about. *She* is the one who's supposed to bring spring, not the Lady. I'm going to try to find her and see if she'll help me, or maybe if I can help her. The land has a stain on it, and I have to get it out."

Yes! That was a very good idea. After the Mór had seized power from the true Lady, Leaf Woman had flown into hiding because she could not live in a land stained by the blood of the Mór's hunts. Fer was right—if she wanted to cleanse the land, she needed to find Leaf Woman. And he knew just where to look for her.

"I really did see her before," Fer said. "In the forest, when I first got here."

That was a very good thing. Come on, Fer, let's go. I'll lead you to her.

"Hold on a second, Rook," Fer said, slinging her backpack and her bow and quiver onto her shoulders. "There's something else."

He trotted back to her.

She crouched down, at eye level with him. "Another reason I came back is because I have to help Phouka. And you too, Rook."

He stared at her. That's a terrible idea, Fer. Don't be stupid.

She reached out her hand and he growled and backed away. With a sigh she got to her feet. "Rook, I don't have much practice at being friends with anybody. But I'm sure that I *am* your friend, and Phouka's. And I'm going to help you whether you like it or not."

For just a second Rook wanted to knock Fer down and bite her to make her pay attention. To help him and his puck-brother she was going to walk right up to the Mór, wasn't she, and then more terrible things would happen.

But he wouldn't bite Fer. Not now, anyway, no matter how much she made him want to.

Rook led the way out of the clearing, pausing at the edge of the path to snuff the wind. No wolves, no smell of pursuit. The Mór would still be hunting him, though. After she had changed him, she'd made the mistake of ordering him, in his dog shape, back to the camp, but not saying he should wait there for her. So he'd done exactly, precisely, as she'd ordered. He'd gone back to the camp to sniff around, then he'd left again and gone into hiding. The Mór's wolves would find him eventually—they always did—but in the meantime he could help Fer.

Fer followed four-legged Rook down a path that got more and more narrow, closing in around them. The sun came up, but the day stayed cloudy gray and damp. After a couple of hours of walking, Fer wanted to stop for a rest, but Rook kept going, trotting ahead, panting.

In the distance, a wolf howled.

Fer's head jerked up, fright tingling through her nerves. The wolf-guards. Rook bounded back to her, growling.

"I'm coming," she told him, then followed as he raced along the path. Another wolf howled, closer. On they ran, as the path grew narrower and branches whipped across Fer's face. She tripped over a root and fell hard, then scrambled to her feet and pelted after Rook.

Finally he paused, waiting for her to catch up. "Okay," she panted. "Keep going."

Instead of racing on, he nudged her leg, pushing her toward an oak tree at the edge of the path. Unlike all the other trees on the hillside, which were winter-dead, the oak had fresh green leaves sprouting from every twig. The tree grew right out of the hillside and its roots grew down to the path, supporting it like thick table legs. From under its moss-draped roots flowed a trickle of water that went across the path and down the hill on the other side.

Fer caught her breath. "We don't have time for a drink, Rook." Two wolves howled, a chorus. Fer's heart gave a little jolt of fright. They were close.

Rook rushed to the tree and pointed his nose under the roots, then looked back at Fer with his ears pricked.

Fer frowned. No, this wasn't about a drink. She crouched and peered under the mossy roots. It was like a cave in there, a hollowed-out place under the tree. She squinted, but all she saw was darkness. When she pulled her head out, she heard the wolves howling louder, closer.

Quickly she ducked into the cave to hide. She crawled farther in, the smell of dirt and moss thick in her nose, water soaking the knees of her jeans. She turned her head to call for Rook to follow when she heard a rumbling growl, right outside the tree. Wolf. Rook needed to hide—now!

She crept back toward the entrance.

Snuff-snuff-snuff.

She froze. A gray-furred muzzle sniffed along the

edge of the cave. One step closer and the wolf would see her, where she was hiding in the dark.

Snuff-snuff.

Then, from farther away, came the sound of a dog barking. The gray muzzle disappeared, and a moment later the wolf howled. Fer heard a rush of wind and paws on the trail as the wolves raced past.

Crouching, she peered from under the tree's roots to see the wolves running down the path, Rook fleeing before them.

Rook was leading them away from her. She had to help him. She started to crawl out of the cave. Then she felt the same tingling in her fingers that she'd felt when she'd opened the Way that brought her from her world into the land. The power grew, and she felt a release, like a door opening, and the ground crumbled away beneath her.

twenty-two

Fer got to her feet. It hadn't been a long fall, just enough to knock the wind out of her when she landed. She was in a cave; its dark ceiling arched above her.

The light in the cave brightened. Fer turned around. Before her lay a rooty, mossy floor; ferns grew out of dark crevices. Beyond that she saw a bright, open space the size of a door, surrounded by ferns. From the door came a breeze, soft and warm.

A warm breeze? The forest she and Rook had been running through had been grim and gray and slipping back into winter.

Fer made her way over the slippery roots to the door and, blinking in the bright light, peered out.

She saw a forest of gray-barked beech trees, tall and

slim, with leaves shivering at the tips of delicate twigs. Shimmering sunlight filtered down through the leaves, and pollen drifted like golden dust through the long, slanting sunbeams. The ground was covered with unfurling ferns and moss and tiny white flowers that glowed like stars.

Catching her breath, Fer stepped out into the forest. It was spring here, but concentrated, as if all the springs that were supposed to follow winter in the other lands were here, waiting to be called forth.

"I came through another Way," Fer whispered. Leaf Woman. This must be her place. Rook had meant for her to come here.

She looked over her shoulder. The oak tree stood there like a broad, green queen among the slender beech trees. Huge roots twined around the cave door.

Fer gulped down a knot of worry. Oh, Rook. What would happen if they caught him? Probably the same thing that had happened the last time the wolves had caught him, only this time she wouldn't be there to save him.

She shook her head. She had to do what she'd come here to do, which was find the Leaf Woman—and find her fast.

Fer turned to face the forest. A few steps away stood a cairn, a moss-covered pile of stones like a marker. Just beyond that, a path wound through the ferns. Shrugging her shoulders under her pack and her quiver and bow, Fer set her feet on the path.

She expected a long walk, because all of her walks through the lands had been long, but the path led to another cairn, then another, and then ended in a meadow surrounded by laurel bushes in full bloom. The white flowers lay like drifts of snow over the glossy green leaves. Fer went to the middle of the meadow and slipped her backpack and bow and quiver from her sore shoulders, setting them down in the soft, knee-high grass.

Taking a deep breath, she looked around. Golden sunlight lay warm across the grass. Bees buzzed in the laurel, making a low, sleepy hum. In the meadow bloomed yellow cinquefoil flowers, and a few tall stands of mullein, and fragrant red clover. Magical herbs, for anybody who knew how to use them and say the right spells.

"Hello," Fer called. The drowsy, humming light swallowed up her words. "Hello!" she shouted again, louder.

Nothing. She wasn't alone, though. *Somebody* was there. She couldn't see anybody, but she had that prickly feeling of being watched.

Fer gnawed at her thumbnail. "I need your help, Leaf Woman," she said to the blooming laurel.

No answer.

"Or maybe I can help you. I'm not going away until you talk to me."

Fer paced through the meadow, worry about Rook

making her stomach jump. Had the wolves caught him? Were they taking him to the Lady?

The sunlight grew more golden as the day grew later. Bees droned in the laurel. Tired after running from the wolves, Fer finally sat down, her back against the cairn in the middle of the meadow. She sighed, so tired, too tired even to dig in her backpack for food. Her eyelids grew heavier and heavier, almost like she was falling under a magical spell, until she fell asleep.

❋ ❋ ❋

Rook raced down the path with the wolves pursuing. He heard panting and looked aside and saw a wolf bounding along beside him. It caught his eye and its fanged mouth leered; a wolf running behind yipped, and the wolf at his side yipped back. Laughing at him.

Stupid wolves. They were under the Mór's orders, but they didn't have to enjoy the chase. Rook swerved and shoved the wolf with his shoulder. The wolf was much bigger than he was, but he caught it in mid-stride; it tripped, crashing into the bushes at the side of the path. Rook raced onward, the breath tearing at his lungs. A wolf nipped at his flank and he tripped, then tumbled to the ground, his paws flailing. He rolled to his feet and the wolves closed in. He backed up, snarling. A wolf darted in, its fangs bared, nipping at him, driving him onward. Rook gathered himself and stumbled on.

❋ ❋ ❋

Fer woke up feeling the chill of evening settle over her like a dewy blanket. Blinking, she sat up. The meadow was full of milky mist, and shadows crept in among the bushes. Overhead, the first stars twinkled in the blue-black sky, and a giant golden moon had climbed above the trees, shedding its light across the meadow.

Fer shivered.

"Cold, are you?" said a voice that seemed to rumble out of the ground around her.

Fer jumped to her feet. She'd heard that deep voice before. "Hello?" She looked around the meadow. "Leaf Woman?"

Bushes rustled behind her. Fer whirled and saw nothing. "Are you there?" she asked loudly.

The bushes rustled again. Fer stepped closer, but saw nothing but leaves and shadows.

"I am here," said Leaf Woman's waterfall voice. "What do you want?"

"I have to fix what is wrong, if I can. The Lady has brought something evil to the land, and it's spilling over into my world too. I have to hurry. Can you help me?"

"The *Lady*," Leaf Woman grumbled. "She is no Lady of the land. She is the Mór, and no better than a carrion crow. She was the true Lady's huntress, and she has spilled blood in her foul rituals. She poisoned the land, and I cannot return there."

Fer nodded. Her suspicions were right—the Lady wasn't the true Lady of the land. "I can go back there," Fer said to the rustling bushes. "I can stop the Mór, if you'll show me how."

Glistening in the moonlight, a clump of bees zoomed across the meadow. Fer followed their flight, and there at the edge, where the grass met the laurel bushes, squatted Leaf Woman. Fer stepped closer to see her better. She looked like a stump, as if she'd just grown up there out of the ground. Her skin was leaf green, shading to darker mossy green in the creases of her elbows and in the wrinkles on her broad face. Oak leaves sprouted out of her head like hair and grew over her chest and belly and hung down over her legs like a dress. Her hands and bare feet were gnarled like tree roots.

Leaf Woman pointed with a sticklike finger. "If anyone can fix what is wrong, it is you, not I. It is your duty and your power. But I will help you, because of your mother. Look." She pointed at Fer's feet.

Fer bent down and picked up the stick Leaf Woman was pointing at. It was straight and had green bark and leaves sprouting from one end. The other end looked as if it had just been broken off a tree. The bark felt cool and smooth under her fingers.

"The Mór made a terrible choice," said Leaf Woman. "She sacrificed all—love, duty, loyalty—for power, and now that power is fading. When you touch her with that green stick, the remainder of her power will leave her. When her wrongs are righted, the blood will be cleansed from the land, and I will return to bring the spring."

Fer stared down at the stick in her hand. *Sacrificed all for power.* The Mór had killed her mother and father, she felt sure. *Their* blood was what stained the land, and the stag's, and all the other creatures the Mór had sacrificed to keep her hold on her power. And she, Fer, was the only one who could fix the wrong that had been done. She held up the stick. "I'm supposed to just walk up and touch her with this?"

"If you truly wish to set things right, you must do this," Leaf Woman said. "And you must hurry. She will be seeking another sacrifice. The spilling of more blood will renew her strength. If she spills that blood in a hunt, her power will grow strong again, and the land will weaken."

Fer felt a jolt of fright. Rook. The Mór was hunting Rook.

Fer whirled and raced out of the meadow.

At the queen oak tree, Fer shoved the green stick into her quiver with her arrows and ducked through the rooty doorway, stumbling over the bumpy floor of the dark cave to the wall in the back. She found roots and crevices and climbed up, her feet and fingers slipping on moss, until she reached a ledge at the top. Catching her breath, she reached out and felt open space—a tunnel. She started crawling. Her shoulders brushed against the dirt walls. The backpack and bow and quiver bumped against the ceiling and dirt sifted down onto her face. Darkness pressed in around her. She closed her eyes and kept going, feeling like a mole digging its way through the ground. Finally she came to a place where her hands reached out and felt nothing. Her fingertips tingled, and she opened the Way.

Taking a deep breath, she leaned forward and slipped off the edge.

She fell through darkness. Dirt folded in around her, pressing up against her face, her arms and legs, covering her like a blanket. She tried to shout, and dirt filled her mouth. With her hands she pushed the dirt away; it moved, like heavy water. Holding her breath, squeezing her eyes closed, she kicked her feet and felt herself moving through the dirt. She reached out again and, like parting curtains, she brushed the dirt aside. Light streamed in. Fer fell into the light, then tumbled down a bumpy slope, out from under the roots, landing on the path before the oak tree.

twenty-three

Rook ran until his paw pads ached, until his breath came in desperate gasps, until his four legs quivered with exhaustion.

As he slowed, the wolves closed in around him, a guard. They forced him into a clearing, where they let him collapse, panting, onto the wiry brown grass.

They waited. His heart pounded with fright, then settled. He was too tired to be frightened. The Mór was within her rights to kill him for tricking her, for running away again. Just so long as she didn't find out about Fer.

The wind grew chillier, a cold that got in under his fur and made him shiver. The gray clouds covering the sky grew thicker. The wolves paced around him, alert. Finally, just as a freezing drizzle began to fall, the Mór came.

She rode Phouka, who stumbled with weariness. She jerked him to a halt. Her people filtered into the clearing behind her, all of them far gone with wildling, dragging themselves on four legs or two, half-covered with fur or feathers or scales, their eyes rolling with fright. The Mór's crows settled in the trees around the clearing, perched like rotting fruit on the bare branches.

Rook got shakily to his four feet. He tried to meet his puck-brother's eye, but Phouka stood with his head lowered, blood dripping from a barbed bridle she'd put into his mouth.

The Mór slid down from Phouka's back. Her stolen glamorie had failed; even her other people could see what he saw, the Mór as she really was. She stood hunched, gazing down at him with eyes that looked like holes burned in old paper. The skin on her face was yellowed, cracking, as if it was about to slide off the bones of her skull. Her hair was dusty black feathers.

The wildling was taking her badly. Her power had held it off for a long time, but now her power was fading. She'd have to make a sacrifice to get it back again. She couldn't just spill the blood of a dumb animal or a half-wild troll; that wouldn't be enough. She'd wanted to bind Fer to her with the hunt, and when Fer had refused to shed blood, she'd wanted Fer herself for her prey. But Fer had escaped.

Rook knew what was coming.

"I will give you a head start," the Mór croaked. She shifted, and to Rook it looked like her knees had bent backward, like a bird's legs. "It must be a good hunt. Now, go." She pointed with clawed fingers at the forest. "Run, my puck. Run."

He fled.

❅ ❅ ❅

Blinking, spitting out dirt, Fer sat up. She was back where she started, in the grim, end-of-winter forest.

Good. That was good. Spring hadn't come to this place, so the Mór hadn't spilled anybody's blood yet.

"Okay, okay," she breathed. She couldn't panic. It wouldn't be too late. She would find the Mór and the hunt. Getting to her feet, she left her backpack—it was too heavy to carry, and she had to hurry. Then she checked that the Leaf Woman's green stick was still in the quiver with the arrows and slung it over her shoulder, then did the same with the bow. Ready.

Leaving the rest of her stuff, she started down the path, back toward the moon-pool. The day was overcast and gray, and an icy drizzle hung in the air, thicker than fog but not quite rain.

Then, way in the distance, she heard something. She

stopped and stood still on the trail, her heart pounding. There it was again, the howl of a wolf. It was followed a moment later by the high, distant call of horns.

The hunt. "Run, Rook," she panted. The thought of him shot down with one of the Mór's black arrows made her heart hurt.

On through the forest she ran. She passed the clearing where she and Rook had camped, and kept going, down the narrow, muddy path. The quiver of arrows and the bow thumped on her back, keeping time with her footsteps and her panting breath.

Wolves howled again, just ahead.

Just before she reached the clearing where the Way and the pool were, Fer skidded to a stop. Catching her breath, she padded forward, her ears pricked. From the clearing came the sound of snarling and bushes thrashing, then the ringing sound of the hunting horn.

Her sneakered feet silent, Fer crept to the end of the path and peered in.

The Mór crashed through the bushes into the clearing, riding Phouka. Across the clearing from the Mór, on the other side of the pool, Rook, a ragged, weary dog, retreated as the three huge wolves advanced on him, snarling.

The Mór looked wild, her eyes glittering, her hair a

crest of tattered black feathers. She jerked Phouka to a stop. The Mór's people lurked in the forest behind her, hovering like ghosts among the trees. The Mór's crows circled overhead, cawing.

Taking a deep breath, Fer stepped into the clearing.

The Mór's head swiveled. When she spoke, her voice came out as a croak. "Gwynnefar."

Fer gasped. The glamorie had failed. The Mór was not beautiful any longer, but a wildling creature, with a sharp, beaky face and hands like withered claws. When she reached over her shoulder to jerk an arrow from her quiver, her arm bent the wrong way, as if her joints were on backward. The Mór clumsily fitted a black arrow to the bowstring. She spoke over her shoulder, giving her people an order. "We have a better prey than the puck. After her."

The Mór's people shifted. Fer saw antlers and feathers and pawed feet. They were all wildling. Yet none of them moved to obey the Mór's order.

Fer took another step into the clearing. She felt the land under her feet, the forest dark and mysterious around her, the sky arching overhead, and she felt the stain like a shadow on the land from when the Mór had hunted before. The land and its people—they *needed* her to do this.

She took a deep, steadying breath. It was time to ask

the question. "What happened to my father and mother?"

"Ah." The Mór flinched, as if Fer had struck her. The Mór's crows dropped out of the air, settling on the tree branches all around the clearing, as if they were waiting to hear the answer.

Fer took a step forward and asked the question again. "What happened to my father and mother?"

The Mór's face went even paler. The clawlike hands holding the bow and arrow shook. "You dare not ask a third time," she croaked.

Yes, she did, she did dare. "I ask you a third time, false Lady. Tell me," Fer said, and she felt the power of command in her voice. "What happened to my father and mother?"

The Mór cried out, a harsh croak of a scream. She spoke the words as if they were being wrenched out of her. "I hunted them. I spilled their blood. I . . . killed them."

Fer spoke past the lump in her throat, trying to keep her voice from shaking. She had suspected, and now she knew for sure how their story had ended. "My mother was your true Lady, and you were her most trusted ally. You were sworn to serve her. You broke your oath."

"I did," the Mór said, her voice the merest thread of a whisper. "And the price has been more than I could pay."

Fer slung the bow from her shoulder. She reached back for an arrow. If she shot the Mór, she could get close enough to touch her with the green stick, as Leaf Woman had told her to do. And the Mór, the usurper who'd taken the true Lady's place—she deserved shooting for what she'd done.

Fer took up her shooting stance and pulled back the bowstring. She sighted down the arrow, aiming it directly at the Mór's heart. The shot settled within her. She closed her eyes, feeling grim and determined.

In the moment of darkness she saw her parents' deaths as the land remembered them. Fer saw the hunt, the chase through the wild night, the moonlight; this time not a stag but Owen and the betrayed Lady, who was really just a girl named Laurelin, who stumbled terrified into the clearing, trying to get through the Way, and the mounted huntress pulling arrows from her quiver, shooting them down before they could escape. Their blood, black in the moonlight, spilling, seeping into the ground. The true Lady's blood shed in a hunt, tainting the land, the source of all the wrongness here.

The Mór had wanted the Lady's power to rule the land and bind her people to her as tightly as if their oaths were chains. And all she had given the land in return was blood and death.

"No," Fer whispered. "I won't shed more blood in this place." Opening her eyes, she lowered her aim, releasing the arrow. It flew across the clearing and buried itself in the ground at the Mór's feet.

A sneer blossomed on the Mór's face. "You are weak, just like your mother. She took the arrow meant for him, but I killed them both, just the same." She groped in her quiver for a black arrow. "And now I will kill you." The crows in the trees cawed out raucous jeers.

Quickly Fer reached into her own quiver, felt under her fingers the leafy end of the green stick that Leaf Woman had given her. She pulled it out and fitted it to the bowstring.

Across the clearing, the Mór's clawlike hands struggled with her own bow and arrow.

Fer sighted down the green stick. The shot settled within her, she felt the rightness, and she let it go. The green stick sped through the air, finding its target.

The Mór flinched as it struck, her hand going to her chest. Her mouth stretched open and instead of a scream, a harsh caw escaped from a sharp beak. The yellowed skin of her face cracked, and from the cracks feathers sprouted, spreading from her forehead, down the back of her neck, across her hunching shoulders. Her hands curled into claws. A flash of brilliant light, and a huge crow tumbled from Phouka's back, then caught itself and flapped upward on ragged-feathered wings. The Mór-crow circled, gathering the crows that had been perched in the trees. They swirled around the clearing like tattered leaves blown by the wind until the Mór-crow gave a shrieking caw and they flew up, higher and higher.

Her heart pounding, Fer watched her go. The Mór and her crows became distant black blots in the gray sky, then a smudge, and then they disappeared.

twenty-four

Fer lowered her bow.

On the other side of the clearing, the black dog that was Rook coughed and spat something from his mouth. The air blurred and Rook's own hand caught the shifter-tooth. The wolves surrounding him growled.

Fer took a few steps toward them. "Behave yourselves," she said, and through her connection to the wolves she felt them tremble at her order.

The wolves cowered away. Fer kept going around the pool. "Rook, are you okay?"

"Oh, sure I am," Rook answered, his voice rough. He stood with his head lowered, the shaggy hair shadowing his face.

From behind her, Fer heard the sounds of others

entering the clearing. She turned to look. The Mór's people came in silently, shivering as the wildling brought on by the Mór's evil left them, as paws turned to feet and horns faded away and fur smoothed into skin. Phouka stood among them on wobbly legs, still a horse.

"What about Phouka?" Fer asked. "Can he change back too?"

Rook rubbed a weary hand across his eyes. "I don't know. He might've been a horse for too long."

"Why did the Mór do this to him?" she asked, now that he was free of the Mór and could answer her questions.

"He's a horse, Fer," Rook growled. "He wasn't able to tell me."

"Rook," she chided.

He gave a half-apologetic shrug. "It is the Mór's punishment for helping your father take you through the Way."

Poor, brave Phouka. Fer nodded, understanding. Rook had been brave too, binding himself to the Mór to save his puck-brother's life. "I think he likes being a horse," Fer said.

"He does, yes," Rook agreed.

Silence fell over the clearing. Fer looked across the round pool, which gleamed like a mirror in the gray light. Burr and Twig stood holding hands; beside them was a badger-man, and a deer-woman; more of the Mór's people stood stunned at the edge of the forest. Another badger-man turned to Phouka and started taking the nasty bridle from his mouth.

What now, Fer wondered. She'd dealt with the Mór and righted the wrongs that had been done. Now what was she supposed to do? It still wasn't spring here, and probably not on the other side of the Way, either.

The people stirred and whispered. A fresh breeze kicked through the clearing, sending ripples across the pool, making the tree branches rattle.

"She's coming," Burr said in a thin voice.

"No, she's here," Twig added.

Fer heard a rustling in the bushes. She turned and saw Leaf Woman, stumpy and green, looking like she'd always been there, like she'd grown up there and had roots deep into the ground.

Without speaking, Leaf Woman stumped across the clearing to the place where the Mór had turned into a crow and flown away. She glanced up at the sky for a second, as if checking to be sure the Mór was really gone, then bent and picked up the green stick from where it had fallen. She held up the stick.

The Mór's people shifted and murmured, then fell silent. Fer felt a touch and almost jumped in surprise as Rook's fingers closed over hers. She glanced aside at him.

"Watch," he whispered, and nodded toward the Leaf

Woman. "This is how it's supposed to be done."

Fer watched.

Still holding the stick, Leaf Woman closed her eyes. She opened them and turned to point the stick in all four directions. Then she took either end of the stick in her hands and cracked it open. The whole forest held its breath. A drop of sap gathered at the broken end of the stick. Shining in the light, the sap dropped slowly down and landed on the dead brown moss.

Fer gasped as she felt, with every part of her, the droplet of sap seep into the ground. The stain that shadowed the land lifted, as if it had never been there at all.

As Fer breathed out again, the forest did too, and spring came rushing in, spreading from the spot where the drop of sap had fallen, the moss turning greener than emeralds. The spring spread farther, leaves popping from the ends of twigs, trees stretching toward the sky, ferns unfurling. A warm breeze rustled the leaves. The gray clouds retreated from the sky and the setting sun shed golden beams across the clearing.

"There," said Leaf Woman with a happy sigh. "That works better than blood, doesn't it?" She dropped the pieces of broken stick on the ground. Around her, the Mór's people were smiling and laughing, and turning their faces like flowers to the golden sun, and some of them were weeping.

Fer took her hand from Rook's and started around

the edge of the pool; Rook followed. One of the Mór's people interrupted her. The wolf-guards had turned back into people.

"Hey-ho, Fer-girlie!" the she-wolf said, grinning. "What're you doing here?"

"Are we finally going to get that toast?" the other guard asked.

"Stupid wolves," Rook's voice muttered behind her.

Fer patted the she-wolf's arm and kept going.

Leaf Woman turned smiling to her as she came up. Her square teeth were stained brown, like wood. "Well, Gwynnefar," she asked in her rumbly voice. "What are you going to do now?"

Fer glanced at the pool in the middle of the clearing. The breeze still blew, but the surface of the water was smooth, reflecting the clear blue of the springtime sky. The Way was open. Fer felt a little knot of sorrow tie itself in her chest. She couldn't leave Grand-Jane alone, but she hated the thought of leaving this land and its people forever and closing the Way behind her.

"Do you know who you are?" Leaf Woman asked.

Fer nodded. "I'm Fer."

The Leaf Woman pointed with one of her gnarled fingers. "What else are you?"

Fer considered the question. She'd used spells and herbs to heal the wildlings. "I'm a healer," she realized. Just like Grand-Jane. And she'd fought off the wolf-guards and saved Rook's life three times. "I'm a warrior, too. And I opened the Way."

"So you did," Leaf Woman said, grinning. "I ask again. What are you?"

Fer took a deep breath. She looked around the clearing, at the half-wild people, at weary Phouka and tricksy Rook, and at the forest beyond. She blinked and saw it again, its magic and splendor and wonder. She felt a fierce urge to guard and protect this land and its people, and to make sure things here were right. *This* was what her mother had felt.

"I know what I am," she said slowly. "I am the Lady of this place."

"You are," Leaf Woman said. She held up her hands and spoke a word, and a crown appeared, a glowing circlet of twigs and budding oak leaves. "Come here and lower your head," Leaf Woman ordered.

Taking a deep breath, feeling the power of the land tingling in her fingers and toes, Fer stepped forward and bowed her head.

Leaf Woman raised the crown. "Lower," she grumbled. "You're a bit taller than I am, Lady."

Smiling, Fer ducked lower, then felt Leaf Woman place the crown on her head. Fer straightened. Around the clearing, all her people bowed, and she felt a web of connection to them, and it felt good, and it felt *right*.

Fer felt a little hope blossom. "Can I go home and see Grand-Jane, and come back here again?"

"The Ways will always be open to you, Lady," Leaf Woman said. "You can."

Then she would. She turned to Rook. "What about you, Rook? Are you going to stay in this land?"

Rook shook the shaggy hair out of his yellow eyes and laughed, and for the first time Fer saw the *real* Rook, the puck unbound, full of sharp-edged mischief. "Maybe I will, Fer," Rook said, grinning. "And maybe I won't."

Oh, Rook. Smiling, Fer stepped up to the edge of the round pool and looked down. The water, mirror bright, reflected a tall, wild-haired girl wearing a patched jacket and carrying a bow and arrows, smiling back at her.

On the other side, spring had come. Grand-Jane would be expecting her; she'd be at the moon-pool, waiting. Fer looked back over her shoulder. Phouka tossed his head and snorted. Rook, among the rest of her people, sketched a wave and grinned.

She waved back. "See you soon," she said.

And she jumped.

Acknowledgments

Many thanks . . .

To my wonderful editor, Antonia Markiet, who shines light into the dark places.

And to the outstanding team at HarperCollins, starting with editor Alyson Day, copy editors Amy Vinchesi and Kathryn Silsand, editorial director Phoebe Yeh, publisher Susan Katz, associate editor Jayne Carapezzi, art director Sasha Illingworth, production supervisor Ray Colon, Tony Hirt, publicist Marisa Russell, and cover artist Jason Chan.

To my agent, Caitlin Blasdell, and her ruthless critiques, ow, ow, ow. And to the Liza Dawson Agency, especially Havis Dawson.

For support and friendship, Ingrid Law. I believe we have a lunch date coming up, my dearest . . . !

Jennifer Adam, who kindly answered all my questions about horses, and about not-horses. Lisa Will, astronomer consultant extraordinaire. Jon Michael Hansen, for the archery info. Deb Coates, the dog whisperer.

To bookseller Beth Yost, from Cover to Cover Children's Books in Columbus, Ohio, who said, upon reading *The Magic Thief,* "Um, I actually like that story you wrote about the changeling girl. . . ." Beth, you inspired me to turn that story into this novel.

To Karen Meisner, Jed Hartman, and Susan Marie Groppi, who bought that changeling girl story and published it at www.strangehorizons.com.

This book's intrepid first readers, Rae Carson, Greg van Eekhout, and Jenn Reese. Also to Dragons of the Corn: Deb Coates, Lisa Bradley, and Dorothy Winsor, and to the memory of Alex Tint. To Iowa City's Nano Rebels, in whose company much of this book was written: Wendy Heinrich, Lori Dawson, Amy Luttinger, Susan Benton, Britt Deerberg, Bev Ehresman, Eleanor Ditzel, Dori Hillestad Butler. To Jessie Stickgold-Sarah, Haddayr Copley-Woods, Robin LaFevers, Kristin Cashore, Charlie Finlay, bookseller Shawna Elder, and to the biggest threat to children's publishing to come along in quite a while, Paolo Bacigalupi.

To all my dear families, especially my vegetarian children, my husband, and my mom and dad.